COOPER'S CHOICE

LAURA SCOTT

READSCAPE PUBLISHING, LLC

Created with Vellum

CHAPTER ONE

Cooper Orchard caught a glimpse of the pretty dark-haired woman walking swiftly toward the church for the second day in a row. He'd noticed her for several reasons—her beauty, her single-minded determination, and the air of fragile innocence that surrounded her. His artistic eye had especially longed to capture the intense expression on her heart-shaped face, which was framed by her dark wavy hair.

Turning over the page of his sketchbook, he continued drawing her likeness from what he'd started yesterday, working swiftly as he suspected she wouldn't be there long. At least, she hadn't been yesterday. As her image bloomed on the page, he found himself wondering why she kept going into the church. Two days in a row seemed like a lot.

Cooper had absolutely no desire to get anywhere near the so-called house of God. After suffering physical and psychological abuse during the five long years he'd been stuck living with the Preacher, he refused to have anything to do with religion. The Preacher's screaming about sin and God's wrath had only reinforced the hell he and his foster siblings had lived in. They'd only managed to escape the seemingly endless abuse because of the fire that had broken out late one night.

The Preacher and his wife, Ruth, had died in the blaze. Personally, Cooper had always thought they'd gotten exactly what they'd deserved. Karma, considering how much the Preacher had screamed at them, hitting them with switches as he ranted about the fires of hell.

Well, the fires of hell had certainly taken the Preacher.

He was so intent on his sketch he didn't notice the woman who approached from his left. "Oh, you do such amazing work," she gushed.

Normally, Cooper would have turned on the charm. After all, he earned a living by sketching tourists, and early August in Gatlinburg was a peak time for business. Women like this lady standing next to him tended to flirt with him, wanting to see their likeness recreated, especially when he made sure their image was more flattering than reality. No wrinkles, no lines, more definition to the cheekbones and jaw. And he always played up their eyes.

Only, today, he found himself irritated by the distraction. He forced a smile. "Happy to sketch you after I finish this one."

"And how long will that be?" She sounded a bit put off. As if he should drop everything to cater to her wishes. Again, something he'd normally do.

"An hour, maybe less." He told himself he was crazy to annoy a paying customer, but he suspected his mystery girl would be coming out of the church again soon. And he wanted to get another look at her so he could finish his drawing.

"I'll see if I can make it back here." The woman who looked old enough to be his mother, if he had one, turned away.

He let her go and continued drawing, one eye glued to the church entrance. When the beautiful woman came out of the church, his heart kicked up a notch. There was something about her that called to him. Some quality he couldn't quite define.

Who was she? Why did she go inside the church these past two days? It was Friday, not Sunday, although he knew some people didn't limit their worship to one day a week. The Preacher who'd tormented him and his foster siblings had done so nearly every day, rain or shine.

A movement behind his mystery girl made him frown. A man wearing black jeans, a black T-shirt, and a black baseball cap pulled low over his eyes stepped out from behind a tree, falling into step just a few yards behind her. A warning tingle shot down the back of Cooper's neck, every instinct going on high alert. He tossed his charcoal stick down and left his easel, stool, and sketchbook to follow them.

At some level, Cooper knew he was taking a risk leaving the tools of his trade behind. After all, drawing was his livelihood. He couldn't afford to replace whatever someone decided to steal. But the man dressed in black appeared to be keeping a keen eye on the pretty woman, and Cooper didn't like it.

He'd lived on the streets long enough to recognize someone with less than honorable intentions when he saw one. When he noticed the pretty woman glancing furtively over her shoulder, he quickened his pace.

The guy in black moved faster too. Cooper instinctively knew the guy intended to grab her. He broke into a run and forcefully rammed into the guy, knocking him off his feet.

"Run," he shouted to the pretty girl as the guy in black scrambled up to take a swing at him.

Cooper ducked and lashed out with his foot, kicking the guy below the belt. Street fighting at its best. The guy in black moaned and doubled over in pain. It was the break Cooper needed.

He rushed forward, irritated to note the pretty girl was still standing there, gaping at him in surprise. He scowled. "I told you to run."

"I—you . . ." She looked badly shaken. She belatedly turned and ran.

Cooper kept pace, covering her back. He could practically taste the girl's fear as she sent furtive glances at him over her shoulder.

"Get away from me," she shouted.

She wanted him to get away from her? What about the guy dressed in black? Cooper was no threat. Not like that guy.

Suddenly another man appeared, stepping out from between two buildings. He was dressed exactly like the other guy, all in black including the same plain black baseball cap. The pretty girl gasped and tried to dart around him, but the stranger reached out to snag her arm. She screamed, and Cooper sprinted forward.

"Let her go!" He punched the guy in the face, causing pain to shoot through his hand and up his arm. Not the smartest move as his hands were his bread and butter. The stranger reared back and must have loosened his hold on the pretty girl's arm enough that she was able to yank free.

Cooper followed up with a kick to his groin, before spinning away and once more following the pretty girl. This time, she seemed relieved to see him.

"This way." Cooper grabbed her hand, tugging her around the corner. He knew this area of Gatlinburg better than most, from living off the streets and working the tourist crowd. He captured the girl's hand, tugging her to a narrow alley between two buildings.

She went along with him, her dark eyes wide with fear. Cooper took every shortcut he could think of to put more distance between them and the two men dressed in black.

He finally led her into a coffee shop located two blocks from his low-budget apartment. He figured the coffee shop would put her at ease more so than taking her to his private digs.

"W-who are you?" she managed when they snagged an empty table away from the window. She straightened the small square purse she wore crosswise over her body.

"Cooper Orchard. Who are you?"

"Mia . . ." She stopped, bit her lip, and glanced away. "Thanks for your help. I should go."

"Wait a minute." He held up his hand. "Shouldn't you call the police? Those guys were about to grab you."

"I-I will." She glanced around nervously. "But this doesn't concern you."

He stared at her. Mia was a pretty name, but he had a feeling it wasn't her real one. Not that he was one to talk. His last name was fake too. As was his ID, driver's license, and social security number. "I think it's a little late for that. I just assaulted two men."

"I'm sorry." Her expression crumpled. "Truly, I feel terrible you had to do that. Thanks for your help, but you should go back to your sketching."

He lifted a brow. "You noticed me sketching?"

She blushed, then frowned. "Go away, Cooper. Leave me alone."

He didn't understand what was going on with her, but no way could he simply walk away. He raked his gaze over her arms, relieved there were no needle tracks marring her skin. Prostitution? Sex trafficking? Maybe.

"Let's head over to the closest police station. They'll help you get away from those guys, find you a safe place to stay."

"I can't." Her voice was a mere whisper.

He swallowed a wave of frustration. "The cops aren't going to arrest you." At least, he didn't think so. Then again, he wasn't sure what she was running from. Had she committed some terrible crime? Armed robbery? Manslaughter?

Murder?

It seemed unlikely, especially since her fear was too real to be faked. She must be a victim. So why not go to the cops?

"You don't understand." She slid off the stool. "Really, Cooper, I'm fine. I appreciate your help. But you're better off staying far away from me."

The smart move would be to let her go. To return to his sketching, hoping no one had stolen his stuff. He had rent to pay. Sitting here with Mia wasn't going to bring in the cash he needed to live off of.

But he couldn't walk away. Not from a woman in distress. "Okay, look. I'll take you to my apartment. You can stay there while I go back for my things. We'll figure out where to go from there, okay?"

Mia shook her head. "You don't know what you're getting into."

No, he didn't. Although it was obvious Mia was running from a couple of bad dudes. Two men he'd assaulted, not that he believed either one of them would report the incidents to the police.

They hadn't tried to take her purse. No, Mia was in

danger, and he couldn't stand the idea of something bad happening to her. It was oddly reassuring that she kept trying to protect him. "I live nearby." He met her gaze. "Don't you think the best move right now is to hide out for a while? Disappear long enough to shake those guys loose?"

She hesitated, clearly torn between wanting to do just that and staying on the move. He could relate as he'd spent several months avoiding the police while struggling to survive. He and Trent had spent several years on the streets before Cooper began using his sketching to make money legitimately from tourists rather than stealing from them.

Sketching didn't pay as well, but he preferred working than running. Trent had gotten involved with a band, and for a while they'd continued to live together. Until the band had moved on to Nashville, taking Trent with them.

It had hurt Cooper to lose the company of his foster brother, but he'd made the best choice for his own well-being. Trent had done the same. He couldn't blame Trent for taking a different path, for wanting something more. Even if that meant leaving Cooper behind.

He shook off the depressing thoughts. "Mia? My place?" It struck him she might be thinking the worst. "I'll sleep on the couch. I promise I won't take advantage of the situation."

"And I should believe you, why?"

He liked the fighting spirit in her dark eyes. "Good point, we really don't know each other. To be honest, there is something I'd like from you."

Her entire body went tense. "No."

He shook his head. "You didn't let me finish. I'd like to sketch you."

She frowned. "Why on earth would you want to do that?"

"I'm an artist, and you're beautiful," he answered honestly. "Just a sketch, nothing more, in exchange for you being able to hide out from those bad guys who tried to abduct you."

She was silent for several long moments. Finally, she nodded. "Okay. A sketch."

"Great." Relief intermingled with anticipation washed over him. Mia had agreed to stay, at least for the night.

Technically, he'd lied about what he'd wanted from her. He wanted to understand what was going on, who she was running from, and why. He also wanted to protect her, which was a bit unusual, especially for someone who'd spent years looking after himself.

But for now, he'd settle for the sketch.

WHAT IN THE world was she doing with Cooper Orchard?

Mia Royce knew she should find a way to ditch him. She was safer on her own. Well, maybe not, but Cooper was definitely much safer without her.

She was the one in danger. She had no right to drag an innocent guy into her problems. Into the mess that was her life.

Yet the chance of having a safe place to stay for a few hours had been too good to pass up. She wanted to believe those two guys hadn't been looking for her specifically, but she was afraid they were. She needed to call her US Marshals contact, Sean McCarthy. He'd come and get her.

They'd spoken on Wednesday, during their regular weekly call. She knew he had other witnesses assigned to him, so having a place to hang out until Sean could pick her up would be helpful.

Still, this shouldn't have happened. Witness protection, better known as WITSEC, wasn't all it was cracked up to be. What if those guys were involved with Frank Germaine? How could they have possibly found her? Especially in this area of the city, which wasn't where her apartment or job was located.

The church?

She inwardly winced at the thought. There was more than one church in Gatlinburg, but if her cover was truly blown, she felt it was possible Germaine's men had watched each of them in an effort to find her.

A tactic that had obviously worked.

Sean had counseled her not to go back to her old habits. That doing such a thing would make it easier for them to find her. And he'd been right.

Yet she needed God's strength and support. Her faith was all she had left. Everyone else was gone. Dead, or gone in a way she'd never see them again.

Lord, I need You. Please keep me safe.

"Mia?" Cooper's voice interrupted her thoughts.

"What?"

"Are you sure about this? I don't want you to be afraid."

It was far too late for that. Germaine's men scared her more than anything on the planet. The irony was that Cooper didn't elicit any fear in her at all. He was a stranger, yet she still wasn't frightened of him. Maybe because she'd seen him sketching on the sidewalk across from the church yesterday and today. She rested her hand on her small bag and glanced toward the window. "You think it's safe to head outside?"

"We'll go out the back, I know one of the kitchen workers." Cooper stood and held out his hand. He was incredibly handsome, wearing his blond hair longer than most men she'd known, his overall appearance being that of a magazine model rather than an artist. His blue gaze was mesmerizing, she'd felt its impact even from a distance.

She took his hand, doing her best to ignore the zing of attraction. This was hardly the time or the place for such foolishness. Her plan was to stay with Cooper long enough to be rescued by Sean McCarthy. She didn't know how long it would take for Sean to get to her, but she could sleep on Cooper's sofa if necessary. Once Sean arrived, she'd be taken to yet another city, provided yet another name.

The idea filled her with despair, but there wasn't another option. She'd testified against Frank Germaine Sr., and Sean McCarthy had recently informed her that Frankie Junior had taken over for his father. She couldn't help but suspect that Frankie Junior was responsible for this recent attempted assault. That Frankie was determined to make her pay.

With her life.

Cooper guided her through the kitchen to the rear door of the shop. She was mildly surprised no one stopped them or asked what they were doing. Cooper must do this sort of thing on a regular basis.

Or maybe he came back here to see his *friend* on a regular basis. There had been two younger women working back there, both very pretty. Cooper looked like the type of guy who could have his pick of women.

He may have called her beautiful, but she knew that was likely a line. Something to convince her to let him sketch her. Maybe he needed practice.

The apartment building was small and could have used

a bit of maintenance. Not that she was living in the lap of luxury these days.

Once, she'd gone to private schools and lived in the largest house in the neighborhood. Before she'd discovered her father was doing business with Frank Germaine. Illegal business.

Criminal activity that had ultimately gotten her father and stepmother murdered. Leaving her as the only witness to the crime.

"It's nothing fancy." Cooper had mistaken her silence for disapproval.

"It's perfect." She smiled. "Thanks for doing this. I really appreciate having a place to hang out for a while."

His gaze bored into hers. "For a while? Will you still be here when I return with my things?"

She hesitated, then nodded. "Yes. I won't lie to you. It's possible my being here puts you in danger. However, I promise I won't leave without telling you." Being honest about this much was the least she could do.

"Okay. Thanks." Cooper waved a hand to the minuscule kitchen. "Help yourself. I should be back within the hour."

"I will." She watched him go, then pulled her disposable phone from her purse. The phone Marshal Sean McCarthy had given her. She made the call, leaving an urgent message.

Her mind went back to those two men who'd tried to grab her. Frankie's men? Or something different?

No, she didn't believe in coincidences. Something was wrong, and she needed Sean's protection now more than ever. She drew in a deep breath, telling herself not to panic. She'd spoken to Sean two days ago. He'd call her back any minute and make arrangements to whisk her to safety.

The US Marshals had assured her she'd be safe with them. Explaining how they'd never lost a witness who followed their rules. The most important being not to contact anyone in her former life.

Not a single person, friend, old college roommate, old boyfriend. No one.

And she had followed their rules. She'd cut off all ties to everyone she'd known back in Chicago. The only rule she'd broken was going to church. It was the one former habit she hadn't been able to stop.

Logically, she hadn't viewed going to church services to be a big problem since her location and identity here in Gatlinburg were supposed to be a secret.

A decision that had backfired in a big way. Her secret location was anything but. Germaine's men had found her. How? She had no clue.

She stared down at her phone, willing it to ring. She'd never had to call Sean in an emergency like this. How long did a response take? She supposed he could be busy with another witness.

Time to stop freaking out. Sean would call her back, and she'd soon be safe. Yet in the back of her mind, she couldn't help but wonder if something had happened to the marshal? Sean wasn't that old, maybe ten to fifteen years her senior, but maybe he had an aneurysm. Or an aggressive form of cancer. A sudden heart attack.

She stood and paced the small length of the room. Every possibility that flashed through her mind was worse than the previous one.

Paranoia gripped her around the throat. Maybe Frankie Junior had found Sean and killed him to get the marshal out of the way. Leaving no one left to protect her. Had they known her contact with the Marshals had been limited to

Sean McCarthy? She knew her name and location were probably on a master list somewhere, but she'd been told to only communicate with Sean. That if Sean got into trouble, he'd send out an emergency notification to a backup marshal.

If something had happened to Sean, how long would it take the backup marshal to reach out to her? A couple of hours? A day? Longer?

She stared down at her phone again, willing Sean to return her call. And if he didn't? She'd have to come up with a plan B.

No way was she going to let Frankie's men find her.

CHAPTER TWO

Cooper ran back to the downtown area of Gatlinburg where he'd left his art supplies. He let out a heavy breath of relief when he saw his things were still there.

No one had stolen them, likely because they didn't hold a monetary value, except to him. It wasn't as if his sketch pad and charcoals could be sold for easy cash. The only person who would be interested in them was another artist.

He quickly gathered his things and stored them in his large knapsack. It pained him to shut down for the day, but he didn't dare linger. Thankfully, he had some cash reserves for days when tourism was low or for when it was raining. On rainy days, he could sometimes set up shop in a small, covered alcove, but not always. And even on those occasions, his income tended to be lower regardless.

Being poor for so many years, never knowing when he'd be able to eat, had made him incredibly disciplined when it came to saving money. He'd vowed never to go without food again.

As he hefted his knapsack over his shoulders, he swept a gaze around the area to make sure the two men dressed in black weren't out there, waiting for him. The older woman he'd put off earlier strode purposefully toward him. "Wait, where are you going?" Her sullen expression indicated she was more than a little irritated.

"Sorry, family emergency." Cooper turned and walked away.

"You told me to come back," she shouted after him.

He had, and normally, he'd have loved nothing more than to take her fifty bucks in exchange for a sketch. But not today.

Cooper made sure to take a circuitous route back to his apartment, just in case the two assailants had in fact been waiting for him to return. He moved quickly and stealthily. Doubling back twice to make sure the men weren't nearby. He finally returned to his apartment, feeling certain he hadn't been followed. When he used his key to open the door, he was relieved to see Mia was still there, sitting on his sofa and staring down at a cheap disposable phone in her hand. She glanced up when he entered.

"That was fast."

He shrugged off the knapsack and set it up against the wall. "Yeah, I was really glad to find no one had taken my stuff."

She flushed. "Me too. I would have felt guilty about that."

"Why?" He arched a brow. "I chose to take off after that guy following you."

"I'm very glad you did," Mia acknowledged. "I wouldn't be alive if not for your quick response."

Alive? The thought made him frown. He crossed over to sit beside her. "You think their intent was to kill you?"

She sighed and put a hand to her temple. "I'm sorry, but I can't talk to you about this."

"Yes, you can," he countered, annoyance lacing his tone. "Can and won't are two different things."

"I know that." She scowled. "Don't lecture me, Cooper. I'm in enough trouble without you adding to it."

"I'm trying to help," he pointed out. "Problems are easier to manage when you have someone on your side. You're saying those two guys were going to grab you and take you someplace to kill you?"

There was a long moment before she nodded. "Yes, that is what my gut is telling me." She lifted her dark, tortured gaze to his. "But please don't ask me about the details. I can't say anything more. I refuse to put you in danger."

He was likely already in danger, especially after assaulting those guys, but he decided to try a different tack. "Please explain to me why you can't go to the police."

She grimaced and looked down at her phone. "Don't worry, I've made the necessary call," she said evasively. "I should hear back from my law enforcement contact soon."

Cooper didn't understand. He thought of the two men, her determination to hide out, and slowly realized what she wasn't telling him. "You're in witness protection."

She looked surprised in a way that confirmed his suspicions. "I didn't say that."

"You didn't have to." A stab of disappointment shot deep. The moment her contact within the program reached out, Mia would be taken away, and he'd never see her again. He swallowed the wave of regret. "Okay, how long until your law enforcement contact calls back?"

"I don't know." She stared down at her phone. "Hopefully soon."

"It's only been ninety minutes."

"True." She forced a smile. "I'm being impatient. I'm sure I'll hear from Sean soon."

Sean? A ridiculous shaft of jealousy hit hard. "Okay, then I guess we'll hang out and wait for a while."

"I owe you for this." Her attempt to smile failed miserably.

"No, you don't. It's the least I can do." He wanted to ask more but sensed there was no point. She wasn't going to tell him anything more.

"You mentioned wanting a sketch?"

Mia's abrupt change in subject had him glancing up in surprise. "Yes, absolutely. But I can wait until you're ready."

"No time like the present." Mia's brisk tone didn't fool him. This was obviously a way for her to uphold her end of their bargain while also having a distraction from the phone call she was waiting for.

"Sounds good." He scanned the room. It would have been better to be outside with the sunlight overhead, but he'd make do with the filtered rays shining through the small living room window. He went over to grab his art supplies, then quickly set up his easel.

"Where do you want me?" Mia was adorably nervous.

"Move over on the sofa a few inches," he instructed. "There, that's perfect." Flipping to a new blank page, he picked up a charcoal, flexed his swollen bruised fingers, and went to work.

"Do I have to smile a certain way or something?"

He grinned. "Not yet. Why don't you tell me something about yourself?"

Her features fell. "I can't."

He eyed her over the edge of his sketchbook. "Sorry, poor choice of words. I meant for you to tell me something about you, Mia. Your hopes, your dreams. What you like and don't like. That's not secret, is it?"

Her gaze turned uncertain. "I guess not."

When she didn't say anything more, he asked, "What's your favorite food?"

"Pepperoni pizza."

"I prefer sausage myself, but pepperoni is good too. Along with mushrooms." He continued drawing.

"One thing I've learned to love is sun tea," she went on. "I never used to like iced tea, but there's something about the way you make it here in Tennessee that makes it delicious."

In some corner of his mind, he registered she must have lived in the north at one point. There was a hint of a Midwest accent in her voice. "Sun tea is great, but lemonade is better."

A genuine smile curved her full lips. "Are you going to argue with everything I like?"

With sure strokes, he captured her smile. "Well, yeah, if you're wrong about something."

"My opinions can't be wrong," she protested.

"Of course they can because my opinions are always right." He was teasing, and she smiled again in response. "What's your favorite song?"

"'I Can Only Imagine' by Mercy Me." Again, she spoke without hesitation.

"Never heard of it." He didn't look away from his sketch, intent on capturing the rapt expression on her face.

"You're missing out. I'm sure you'd love it."

He didn't answer, not really caring about the song, but concentrated solely on the sketch that was beginning to come alive. Cooper barely noticed that Mia had stopped talking, his laser-sharp focus centered on his drawing. Despite his bruised and painful knuckles, it was as if there was a shimmering connection between them, a force that was moving his charcoal over the page with very little effort.

This didn't happen often, but on those rare occasions when it did, he rode along as if he were a surfer gliding over a perfect wave. He honestly had no idea how much time had passed when he finally put the charcoal down and rubbed his aching hand. It had been a long time since he'd been forced to brawl. *Note to self—punching people hurts.*

"Finished?" Mia asked.

He blinked, nodded. "Sorry about zoning out like that." He stood and turned the sketch toward her. "What do you think?"

She drew in a swift breath. "Oh, Cooper. It's beautiful, but I'm sure I don't look like that."

"Yes, you do." He tipped his head to the side. "You're beautiful, Mia. Why do you think I wanted to sketch you?"

"Because I have interesting features?" She continued staring at the sketch. "You are incredibly talented."

Her praise warmed his heart. "Thanks, but it's easy when you have an exceptional model to work with." He glanced at his drawing. "And now that I look at this, black and white doesn't do you justice. I'd love to do another in color."

"Another one?" She shook her head. "You must really need the practice."

Practice? "What are you talking about?"

She looked confused. "I thought your sketching me was for practice. Or I could pay you, depending on how much you charge."

"I didn't sketch you for practice or money." He squelched the flash of hurt. "You're beautiful, but there's more to it than that. You captured my attention yesterday when you went into the church. I knew then and there I needed to draw you. In fact, I started one yesterday and was planning to finish it this morning, before I realized the guy in black was following you."

"Really?" She appeared surprised by that revelation.

He glanced again at the sketch. It was pretty high on his list of best works, if he did say so himself. "I'll let you have this one, if you sit for me again so I can do one in color."

"If that's what you'd like, and if I'm here long enough, I'm happy to help." She smiled. "Although I still think you've created a more flattering image than I deserve."

It wasn't, at least, not the way he did for tourists who were paying for their likeness.

This sketch of Mia had come from something deep within him. Something he couldn't name.

He barely knew the woman, so why did he have this strange connection with her? Especially a woman who went to church? Cooper hadn't dated anyone steadily for a long time. Not that he hadn't had opportunities, because women often sought him out. He figured it was something about his being an artist. Women were drawn to that aspect of his life.

But he'd never talked about his past. About his life with the Preacher. About the abuse he and his foster siblings had suffered.

Looking at Mia, he tried to understand why he was so drawn to her. Not just her beauty but her. Partially, he suspected, because her past might be similar in some respects to his. Maybe even worse than his, considering two men had just tried to grab her. Maybe even to kill her.

The thought brought out every protective instinct he possessed. Anyone trying to hurt Mia would have to go through him.

He opened and closed his injured fingers, knowing he'd throw as many punches as necessary to keep her safe.

And deep down, Cooper found himself selfishly hoping

the phone call Mia was waiting for didn't come anytime soon.

MIA WAS in awe of Cooper's talent and wondered why he was working the sidewalk, drawing for tourists instead of attending an art school. Clearly, he was only making enough to get by, based on the clean yet sparse apartment, yet she felt certain his talent would be enough to get him a scholarship into an art program.

The School of the Art Institute in Chicago would benefit from having a student like Cooper. With his talent, there was no limit as to what he could do or where he could go.

Her stomach rumbled loud enough for Cooper to hear. She blushed and put a hand over her abdomen. "Sorry, I didn't have breakfast."

"You should have said something sooner." He set the sketch aside. "I lose track of time while I'm working, but it's well past noon. Come on." He gestured toward the door. "Let's go find a place to eat."

She hung back. "I don't know, what if those two guys are still nearby? They might easily find us."

He considered her words. "You're right, they may. I made sure I wasn't followed from the sidewalk where I left my supplies, so we're safe here. But it's also a beautiful day, you don't want to spend the rest of it stuck inside. There's a small restaurant I know called Serendipity. It's located well off the beaten path. They have a nice outdoor patio, and I can get you there without walking along main roads."

She loved the idea of sitting outside, and Cooper had gotten her away from the two men in black by taking roads and alleys she hadn't known even existed. She'd been staying in Gatlinburg for over three months, but circumstances had forced her to keep to herself.

It was why she'd taken the risk to go to church. She hadn't even attended a true service, the way she'd wanted, but had gone in to feel closer to God as she prayed.

"Mia?"

She glanced down at her still silent phone, then nodded slowly. "Okay, let's do it."

"I'd like that." He held out his hand. It was no hardship to take it, drawing strength from his warmth.

Cooper led the way outside. The sun was hot, the air humid. Coming to Gatlinburg had been a huge change from the cooler temperatures of Chicago, but she'd enjoyed the temperate weather, the beautiful misty Smoky Mountains, along with the quaint, if tourist-laden town.

In Chicago, she hadn't known her neighbors other than to wave hello from a safe distance that didn't invite conversation. There was no standing around and chatting about life the way most people did here. Even those who were obviously tourists stopped to talk.

At first, she'd been concerned about standing out from the rest, being too conspicuous when she needed to blend in without being noticed. She even tried to pick up a hint of the southern accent, despite knowing she probably wasn't fooling anyone who actually lived here. Thankfully, there were so many tourists year-round that she'd soon realized she wouldn't attract undue attention.

Yet, it seemed likely Germaine's men had found her.

Watching Cooper work had filled her with a sense of peace. He was the beautiful one, not that he'd appreciate being labeled as gorgeous.

His blond hair, lightened no doubt by the Tennessee

sun, had fallen around his face as he'd worked. He had high chiseled cheekbones and a lean, muscular physique. His blue eyes were so incredibly intense she'd felt as if he could look right through her.

Seeing every one of her darkest secrets.

A troubled past she could never share. Even being with her for a short time exposed him to danger.

But she didn't know what else to do. Returning to her apartment didn't seem smart. Neither did reporting in for work. She wanted to check her phone again but left it in her purse.

Cooper took her through a small parking lot and through yet another alley. It made her wonder how many times he'd taken this path, a shortcut to what must be one of his favorite places to eat.

Serendipity. It was a strange name for a restaurant, but she rather liked the sentiment. It described her meeting with Cooper. Ironic that she'd noticed him long before he'd come charging to her rescue. Only to discover he'd noticed her too.

"The restaurant is up ahead." Cooper gestured with his right hand, giving her a glimpse of his red and swollen knuckles.

"We should have iced your hand."

He shrugged. "I'm fine. I sketched you without a problem."

"Thanks again for saving my life." She owed Cooper a debt she could never repay. Sitting for him so he could draw was the least she could do.

"No reason to thank me, I only did what anyone else would have." He hesitated, then added in a low voice, "I don't appreciate men who hurt women."

She shivered despite the sun. He sounded as if he were

speaking from experience. "I personally don't understand why people hurt each other in general. Men shouldn't kill other men either."

"Sounds as if you saw something you shouldn't have."

His keen observation, the second one today, made her stumble. He tightened his grip on her hand, preventing her from falling to the ground. "You have to stop doing that."

"Doing what?"

"Guessing the reasons about why I'm in trouble." She dug in her heels, forcing him to stop.

"I'm good," he said flippantly.

"You're going to get yourself killed," she shot back. "If those guys think I told you everything I know, they'll silence you too."

He held her gaze. "I think I'm already on their hit list simply because I helped you escape by fighting them off. Protecting me from what you know isn't going to change anything."

"You don't know that." Her protest was weak because, deep down, she feared he was right. If those were Germaine's men, which seemed likely, then they would go after Cooper just because he'd helped her escape.

"On the other hand, you talking to me, explaining what's going on, may help release some of the tension you're carrying on your slim shoulders," Cooper went on.

"Thanks, but I have God's help for that."

A look of revulsion crossed his features, but he simply asked, "Is that why you went into the church two days in a row?"

"Yes." She was sad and a bit depressed by his reaction. "I feel closer to God in church."

"Hmm." Cooper broke off eye contact with her, gesturing to the restaurant. "Time to feed you."

She understood he'd changed the subject because he didn't want to discuss God or faith. If she'd be staying in Gatlinburg, she'd try to talk to him about why he didn't believe, but the moment Sean returned her call, she'd be leaving for good.

Never to return.

The restaurant was small but busy. It looked like the kind of place frequented by the locals rather than catering to tourists. Cooper waved to one of the female servers as he led her to the only empty table on the patio.

"Good timing." He grinned.

"Very." She noticed the server he'd acknowledged made her way over.

"Coop, it's been a few weeks." She kissed his cheek, then eyed Mia as if sizing up the competition. "I've missed you."

"Gotta hit the tourist business while it's hot." Cooper turned toward her. "Rachel, this is Mia."

"Nice to meet you," Rachel said with forced politeness. "Are you in town long?"

"No, this is a short visit," Mia said. She didn't want this woman to think she was poaching her boyfriend.

"Hopefully not too short," Cooper protested, obviously clueless about Rachel's feelings.

Rachel's smile slipped. "What can I get you to drink?"

"Sun tea," Mia and Cooper said at the same time.

Cooper chuckled, but Rachel was not amused. Still, she pointed at the chalkboard sign propped against the side of the building. "That's our menu, let me know what you'd like. I'll be back soon with your sun tea."

"Thanks." Mia watched her walk away, then elbowed Cooper. "What's wrong with you?"

"Huh?" He appeared confused. "What are you talking about?"

"Rachel really cares about you."

"We're good friends." For an artist with amazing observations skills, he seemed obtuse about women's feelings. "I care about her too."

"Not in the same way she cares about you—" She broke off further conversation because Rachel returned with their tea.

They ordered their meals. Mia was surprised at how quickly their food came out. She bowed her head to silently give thanks, hyperaware of Cooper's gaze.

She quickly took a bite of her chicken sandwich, glad to have food in her belly. For several minutes, they didn't talk but simply enjoyed their meal.

"I know Rachel would like to be more than friends," Cooper finally admitted in a low voice. "But I don't feel the same way."

She eyed him curiously. "Because you care about someone else? You haven't mentioned a girlfriend."

"No girlfriend." He lifted his blue gaze to hers. "I've been on my own for a long time."

"I see," she said, although she really didn't.

They were silent for long moments. Cooper seemed lost in thought before he began to speak.

"I was stuck for five years in a pretty bad foster home. I was there with six other foster kids." He swallowed hard. "We lived with a man who referred to himself as the Preacher and his wife, Ruth. The Preacher made us kneel for hours, hitting us with a switch while screaming about God and how we were all going to hell for being sinners."

"Oh, Cooper." She reached out to grasp his hand. "I'm

so sorry you had to suffer like that. God isn't mean or spiteful. He is good and kind and loving."

"You can believe what you like," Cooper acknowledged. "But I'm not interested in hearing about it. I don't like to talk about my past, but I wanted you to know why I'm not into praying."

His statement broke her heart. but based on what he'd experienced at the hand of a man who was supposed to be one of God's humble servants, she could understand why. "Thanks for sharing your experience, Cooper. I'm sure that wasn't easy."

The corner of his mouth tipped up into a crooked smile. "No, it's not. You're the first one I've ever talked to about this."

His admission made her feel special. "You can talk to me anytime, Cooper. I'm always willing to listen."

He nodded and took another long drink of his sun tea.

"How did you manage to get away? Did you age out of the foster system?"

"No." He stared down at his glass. "A fire broke out one night. I'm not really sure what happened, but I know Darby woke us up. I could smell the smoke, even in the cellar. Sawyer went up the stairs, and somehow Jayme was there holding the door open. All seven of us managed to escape." He looked at her. "But not the Preacher or his wife. I have a feeling the fire grew out of control partially because of my sketchbook and oil paints. They were Christmas gifts from the church members that the Preacher surprisingly let me keep. I'd spilled some of the paint and left them in the living room, which seemed to be the source of the fire."

News of the fire was shocking. "I hardly think your art had anything to do with the fire," she protested.

He shrugged. "I can't figure out any other reason why

the fire could have gotten so far out of control. Especially since the Preacher and his wife slept in a room off the living space. The smoke should have woken them up. Or the noise of all of us kids coughing and scrambling out of there."

"I'm sure they must have slept very soundly." Mia tried to reassure him. "Did you get sent to another foster home after that?"

"No. We all vowed we'd never go back into the system. We scattered in opposite directions to find a way to survive. Sawyer, Trent, and I went one way, Hailey and Darby went another, Jayme the oldest took care of Caitlyn, the youngest. We lived in the woods, then on the streets." A closed expression settled on his face. "I don't know why I'm telling you all this. It's not pertinent to what's going on with you."

The thought of a young Cooper living on the streets made her feel sick to her stomach. He'd suffered so much while she'd lived in the lap of luxury.

Plush surroundings purchased with ill-gotten gains, but she hadn't wanted for anything. Once her father and step-mother had been murdered, the US Marshals Service had taken over providing for her. She hadn't needed to scrape by simply to survive.

Not compared to Cooper.

A movement from outside the patio caught her attention. She glimpsed a man wearing a black T-shirt and base-ball cap standing several feet behind Cooper's right shoulder. She couldn't see his face, but she didn't dare take a chance. She ducked down, reaching out to grab his arm. "I think they may have found us."

To his credit, Cooper didn't ask any questions. He tossed cash onto the table and rose. "Follow me."

She lost sight of the guy in black as she followed Cooper

swiftly across the length of the patio. He went inside the restaurant, then like last time ducked into the kitchen.

Mia stumbled after him, ignoring the startled expressions on the staff's faces as they went by. How had Germaine's men found them at the Serendipity restaurant? It didn't make any sense. Had Frankie's men stumbled across them by accident? Or had they been followed? Or was the guy simply a tourist who liked to wear black?

She didn't know. All she could do was pray with all her heart that God would keep them both safe.

CHAPTER THREE

Ignoring Rachel's startled and hurt expression, he led the way out the back of the restaurant. He hadn't seen the man in black, but even if Mia was mistaken, he wasn't about to take a chance.

Keeping a tight grip on Mia's hand, he wound his way through the back streets behind the restaurant. When he came to an intersection, he thought it might be good to take one of the busier streets in order to blend in with the tourist crowd.

"How much money do you have?" Cooper asked as they hurried along a sidewalk lined with various shops.

"Maybe two hundred dollars," she responded. "Why?"

"We need to buy a few hats." He tugged her into a shop. "Something with a broad brim for you and maybe a baseball cap for me."

"What good will hats do?"

"They'll hopefully make us look like tourists." He picked up a wide-brimmed straw hat and plunked it on her head. He found a Gatlinburg baseball hat and carried it to the counter. "How much are these two?"

The woman named a price that made him wince. He should have stocked up with cash at his place. He glanced at Mia. "I'm sorry, but I'm ten bucks short."

"Here." She quickly opened her small purse and pulled out a twenty.

After paying for the hats, he glanced around, wondering if they should splurge on T-shirts. He decided against it, knowing he had several at his apartment.

Taking Mia out to lunch had been a mistake. He should have known better. Once they'd returned to his place, he'd make sure they stayed inside until her law enforcement contact returned her call.

And why had he spilled his guts about the Preacher? Was it because he knew she wouldn't be in his life for very long? Ships passing in the dark? Maybe, although he hadn't planned on telling her. On telling anyone.

But her praying had caught him off guard.

And talking to Mia had been surprisingly easy.

He forced himself to concentrate on the issue at hand. "Okay, we're going to ease into the crowd," he instructed as they left the shop wearing their hats. "We need to look like a tourist couple here to sightsee."

"I can do that." Mia's voice was faint, as if she were holding herself together with an effort. Instead of taking her hand, he looped his arm around her waist.

He felt her tense for a moment before she relaxed and did the same. Her slender arm around his waist made him wish this was for real rather than a fake romance to make them look like a young couple intent on touring the area.

This strange attraction was getting annoying. He'd always appreciated beautiful women, it was part of being an artist. But this was oddly different. He'd already sketched Mia once but found himself compelled to do so again.

And worse, he was beginning to realize even one more sketch of her wouldn't be enough.

Just like spending less than twenty-four hours with her wouldn't be enough.

He lowered his head toward her to speak softly into her ear. "See either of our buddies?"

"Not yet." She'd relaxed a bit as if realizing that hiding in plain sight might just work. "Maybe I imagined things."

"Or maybe we simply lost them." Cooper forced himself to stroll leisurely along while keeping his gaze sharp for any sign for either of the two men. "We're going to turn right at the next intersection, then hop on the trolley."

"Okay." She seemed content to allow him to take the lead. How long had she been in Gatlinburg anyway? Most of the locals knew their way around, it wasn't as if Gatlinburg was a huge metropolis. Those who lived and worked in the area knew how to avoid the highly packed streets.

Yet Mia didn't seem as familiar with the area. Where did she live? What did she do? He wasn't usually this curious about people's lives, but he couldn't deny the intense desire to know everything about Mia.

Mia, the woman who hadn't trusted him with her last name, even the fake one assigned by the Feds.

He drew her into the crowd waiting for the trolley. When they were on board, he stayed in the middle, holding on to the pole overhead.

"I've never taken this ride," Mia said, glancing out wistfully.

"Trust me, I don't make a habit of it. But we're tourists, remember?"

Her lush mouth curved into a half smile. "Yes, we are."

Cooper forced himself to look away, afraid he'd succumb to temptation and kiss her. Honestly, this wasn't at all like him. He didn't get emotionally involved with women. Kept himself aloof from emotional entanglements.

His primary goal was to look out for himself. It sounded selfish, but it had been necessary to survive. And now he'd been independent for so long he didn't know any other way to live. Getting close, sharing intimate information, becoming dependent on someone else wasn't part of his plan.

He'd lost a small part of himself when Trent had taken off for Nashville three years ago. He'd never blamed his foster brother, but that didn't mean Trent's leaving hadn't hurt.

This *thing* with Mia was temporary. The idea of her leaving bothered him. Yet, he also knew it was for the best.

He wasn't built for long-term relationships. Which was why he'd refused to get involved with Rachel, despite how much she'd tried to change his mind. He and Trent had once been love 'em and leave 'em kind of guys. They'd broken a slew of hearts as they went along.

Now, rather than breaking hearts, he simply avoided complicated relationships from the very beginning. His art was all he needed.

Or so he thought.

"This is our stop." He wrapped his arm around her waist again. "Get off on the other side from the one we jumped on, okay?"

"Okay." Mia did as instructed, and he quickly followed. Within minutes they were swallowed by another crowd of tourists.

Cooper continued along until they reached the end of the main drag. At that point, he led the way through the back streets to approach his apartment from the opposite side.

"I feel exposed," Mia whispered.

He understood her sentiment. "We need to stay alert."

She gave a jerky nod and swept her gaze around the area.

Cooper felt certain they hadn't been followed. Then again, he hadn't noticed anyone following him prior to being discovered at the restaurant. Had she imagined seeing one of the guys who'd attacked her? Or had they stumbled across their location by accident?

Neither option seemed likely. What mattered now was that he didn't see the assailants.

They finally reached his apartment, almost a full hour from when they'd left the restaurant. He unlocked the door, ushered Mia inside, then closed the door and shot the deadbolt home.

Mia took her hat off and ran her fingers through her dark wavy hair. "That was close."

"I'm sorry." He removed his baseball cap too and raked his too long hair from his face. "I was an idiot to have taken you out for lunch."

A strange sound came from her throat. She slapped her hand over her mouth, but the gurgling noises continued. It took a moment for him to realize she was laughing.

"What's so funny?"

Mia shook her head, obviously trying to get herself under control. "Don't you realize how absurd it is for you to apologize for taking me out to lunch?"

A reluctant smile tugged at the corner of his mouth. "Well, when you put it like that, I guess it did come out wrong."

She controlled her laughing long enough to collapse onto the edge of the sofa. "Oh, Cooper. I don't know what to do." She pulled her phone from her purse. "I have a sick feeling about this. I've never called Sean in an emergency, but I can't imagine why it would take him so long to respond."

He sat beside her and cradled her hand in his. "We can still go to the police. Surely they have a way to call the US Marshals. There has to be someone else who can be contacted to protect you."

"Maybe." The shadow of fear in her dark eyes squeezed his heart. "But what if I choose the wrong cop?"

He frowned. "What do you mean, the wrong cop?"

She let out a heavy sigh. "Something happened to me several months ago, and like every other law-abiding citizen, I went to the police. I thought they'd protect me, but it turned out the cop I spoke to was on the bad guy's payroll." He felt a shiver ripple over her. "It's only thanks to God's grace that I managed to escape. After that, I decided to go straight to the FBI, who in turn handed me over to the Marshals Service."

Cooper had spent many years hiding from the cops, but thankfully, he hadn't run into any bad ones. Cops that were jerks, yeah, but not bad in the way Mia had described. "I understand your concern, but you've been relocated far away from the dirty cop, right? What are the chances that you'd run into another one here in Gatlinburg?"

"I'm afraid to find out." Mia's tone was blunt. "I have no idea how wide and deep this criminal organization is."

She was describing a mafia type of organized crime. But that sort of thing didn't happen in Gatlinburg.

Did it?

"I don't mind having you stay here with me," he said softly. "Let's give Sean a little more time."

"Okay." Mia didn't look convinced. "I would rather go

with Sean, a man I trust, rather than talking to strangers about my situation."

He wanted to reassure her, but he didn't know anything about the criminals she was running from. Organized crime sounded serious. "I'm here for you, Mia."

She dropped her gaze to their clasped hands. "That's twice now that you've saved my life. I'm really worried that those men will continue to hunt you down long after I'm gone."

Gone. His heart squeezed painfully, but he pushed the depressing thought away. "I'm glad I could be there for you."

A tremulous smile curved her lips. "Me too."

He wanted to sketch her again so badly. Almost as much as he wanted to kiss her. He refused to cross that boundary. The last thing he wanted to do was to make her feel uncomfortable staying here with him.

He'd promised her no strings. A platonic arrangement. And he'd meant it. He'd didn't plan to repeat the mistakes in his past. Mia deserved better.

"I think it's time for another sketch." He released her hand and stood. "Before we lose the afternoon light."

"If that's what you'd like," Mia agreed.

He'd like far more and almost drew her up and into his arms. How he'd managed to resist, he had no idea. Cooper took a step back, glancing around the room.

Focus, he told himself sternly. "I'd like you to sit here." He gestured to a different spot on the sofa than where she'd been earlier.

"All right." She scooted over to the area he'd indicated.

Cooper turned to set up his stool, sketchbook, and easel. He opened his box of colored chalk and took a moment to decide where to start.

Once again, he rubbed his sore knuckles, then went to work. As he drew, he was struck by the look of longing in Mia's dark eyes.

The same longing that was mirrored deep within him too. A longing for something they could never have.

———

MIA TOLD herself to get over her fear and to allow Cooper to take her to the closest police station. He was right. The likelihood of a Gatlinburg cop being on Frankie Germaine's payroll was slim to none.

This dependency she had on Cooper wasn't healthy. He wasn't a surrogate for Sean McCarthy. It wasn't Cooper's job to protect her. Yet she was having trouble keeping a safe, emotional distance from him.

His intense gaze as he sketched was mesmerizing. Mia knew she could watch him for hours. Had in fact done that earlier today.

She wasn't an artist, but if she were, she'd want to draw Cooper. He had the most arresting features of any man she'd ever met. She'd dated a few good-looking guys at Northwestern University where she'd initially gotten a degree in fine arts, only to decide to go back to study biology with a plan to go into the medical field, but none who could come close to Cooper's attractiveness.

Get a grip, she ordered herself sternly. She was acting like a silly adolescent schoolgirl rather than a twenty-five-year-old woman.

A woman who'd been living a lie in Gatlinburg for the past three months. Oh, how she'd longed to tell Cooper everything about herself.

A foolish, selfish thought. Hadn't she put the poor guy in enough danger?

If Sean was right, Frankie Germaine was more ruthless than his father. Witnessing Frank Senior shoot her father and stepmother in cold blood had been awful enough. What Frankie Junior had in mind for her was unimaginable.

Her thoughts drifted back to that fateful day. Mia had come home for her father's sixtieth birthday bash a day earlier than planned. She'd been up in her room when she'd heard muffled shouts. After making her way down the stairs to the study, she'd recognized Frank Senior's voice. He'd been introduced at a charity function as her father's business associate.

She'd been out of sight when Frank had pulled a gun and shot her father and then her stepmother. Mia had stood frozen for what seemed like forever before easing silently away from the study. She'd slipped through the house, headed out through the back, much the way Cooper had done in the restaurants, and had ran as fast as she could down the street. There had been a squad parked just a couple of blocks away, so she'd rapped on the cop's window for help. He'd lowered his window, told her he was in the middle of something, and couldn't be bothered, until she'd told him her name. Instantly, he'd told her to get into the squad right away.

The tiny hairs on the back of her neck had risen in alarm. The way he'd recognized her name, the way he'd first tried to get her to leave but then wanted her inside his squad had seemed wrong. She'd turned and ran, firmly believing God had been watching out for her.

The cop had followed, red lights and all, but she'd dodged through several streets and happened upon a taxi.

This time she'd asked the driver to take her to the FBI office, rather than to the police station, where she'd gotten the help she'd needed.

Was she just being paranoid about heading to the Gatlinburg police? Probably.

Mia made a mental promise to ask Cooper to take her to the police station as soon as he'd finished his drawing. The sooner she was out of his apartment, and his life, the safer he'd be.

Yes. She swallowed hard. If Sean hadn't returned her call by the time Cooper was done, she'd go to the police.

It was the right thing to do.

"Mia?"

His low husky voice sent a shiver of awareness down her spine. She looked at him. "Do you need me to move a certain way?"

"No, but you look sad." His gaze held hers. "What are you thinking about?"

"Nothing." *Everything.* "I'm sorry. I'll try to smile."

He shook his head. "No need, I managed to capture your expression before you drifted away into sad thoughts."

His keen observation was unsettling. "How much longer until you're finished?"

"Not long." He smiled. "What's wrong, getting tired of sitting in one spot?"

"No, unfortunately, I sit all day long." The comment slipped out before she could catch herself. She really, really needed to keep her guard up around Cooper. "But I could use a bathroom break."

"Oh, sorry." He looked contrite. "Go ahead."

The apartment was small, so it was easy enough for her to find the bathroom. There were only two doors, and one was hanging ajar, providing a glimpse into his bedroom. She found it surprisingly neat and tidy. Maybe it was a stereotype, but Cooper being a guy and an artist, she'd expected to find a mess.

After using the facilities, Mia took a moment to freshen up. Being the center of Cooper's attention made her feel self-conscious about her appearance. Her nose looked pink from the sun, but otherwise, she was her same unexciting self.

Audrey, her stepmother, had been stunningly beautiful and constantly tried to get Mia to glamour up. As if Mia's everyday appearance was somehow lacking. Looking at her reflection now, Mia couldn't figure out why Cooper had been so set on sketching her image.

Not that it mattered. She wouldn't be here long enough for it to matter. Even a simple friendship was out of the question. Once Sean had relocated her to another city, she'd never be able to reach out to Cooper again.

When she emerged from the bathroom, she found Cooper still at work. Since he didn't seem to need her to continue sitting for him, she went around to see what he'd done.

As before, he'd drawn her features in a way that actually made her look stunning. An image that Audrey would have wholeheartedly approved of. Adding the colors had given her a bolder, brighter dimension.

And the look of longing in her eyes made her realize Cooper had captured exactly how she felt about the situation.

"Wow," she murmured. "You're looking at me through rose-tinted glasses."

"I'm not." There was an edge to his tone, but he didn't look away from what he was doing. "I don't know who did a number on your self-confidence, Mia, but stop putting your-self down. You deserve better."

Ouch. His comment stung, but deep down she knew he was right. She was one of God's children and therefore beautiful. She'd always considered herself to be more attrac-tive on the inside as compared to her outward appearance.

A long silence hung in the air between them. Cooper finally dropped the square stick thing he was using to draw and flexed his injured fingers. "I'm sorry." He glanced at her. "I shouldn't have snapped."

"No, you were right. I—well, I thought I'd overcome my issues, but apparently not as much as I'd like." She gave him a look of admiration. "You're incredible. Your talent is wasted doing sidewalk sketches. You should be in a premier art program."

"Not interested." His curt tone did not invite discus-sion. Hmm. Now who had a self-confidence issue? She wasn't the only one.

"The art world's loss," she said lightly. "Listen, Sean still hasn't returned my call, so we probably should head out to talk to the police. It's obvious something has gone wrong."

Cooper raked his hand through his hair, pulling the long strands from his face. "Are you sure you don't want to wait until tomorrow?"

She grimaced. "I wanted to honor my commitment to you by sitting for your sketch, but staying here any longer isn't smart. We don't know if or how the bad guys found us at the restaurant. I'm concerned they'll find a way to track us here."

"I don't see how they could," Cooper said with a frown.

She was growing exasperated with him. "How many of the local shop owners know you by name? If those guys went around asking for the sketch artist that was recently sitting across from the church, I'm pretty sure someone will tell them what they want to know."

Cooper rose to his feet. "Knowing my name is different from finding out where I live."

"These guys are not amateurs." Her voice rose with annoyance. "Don't you get it? These guys have connections you and I don't. Trust me, these guys want to find me very badly."

"Yeah, I think I figured that part out for myself." Cooper sighed and softened his tone. "Fine. If you want to go to the police station, I'll make sure you get there safely."

"Thank you." She glanced again at the sketch. She doubted she'd ever meet anyone else who looked at her the way Cooper had, and it pained her more than she wanted to admit to leave him behind.

Yet she desperately needed him to be safe.

She cleared her throat and forced a smile. "We should go."

"Okay, just give me a minute." He disappeared into the bedroom for five long minutes before returning to the living room. He'd changed his clothes and approached with a T-shirt in his hand. "Will you change into this for me? It's dark blue and won't be as noticeable as the pink blouse you're wearing."

She took the soft shirt from his fingers. "Sure. I see your point, but I didn't expect to be on the run from bad guys when I dressed this morning."

"Of course you didn't," Cooper agreed. "But the small things we can do to change our appearance might help."

"Okay." Mia took the shirt into the bathroom. She stripped off her pink blouse and donned his dark T-shirt. It was large on her and carried his musky scent.

She held the fabric to her face, inhaling deeply. Feeling

foolish, she straightened, looped her handbag across her chest, and finger-combed her hair. Enough mooning over the guy.

After draping her pink blouse over the edge of the tub, she left the bathroom. Carrying it was impractical, and Cooper could either pass it along to a friend or toss it into the garbage.

"Ready?" His aquamarine gaze warmed when he saw her.

"As much as I can be." She squelched the flash of nerves as she put on her hat.

Cooper donned his baseball cap and led the way outside. When he placed his arm around her waist again, she was secretly glad. If pretending to be a couple worked, she was all for it.

This time they took several different streets, and she trusted Cooper's ability to get her to the police station. Still, she continued raking her gaze over the area, searching for any sign of the two guys who'd attacked her.

"The police station is just a few blocks from here." Cooper's voice rumbled near her ear. "But we're going to head around the back, just in case."

"Okay." She had to admit that he was better at evading bad guys than she was. Likely from the time he'd lived on the street. She was grateful once again for his expertise.

Cooper turned into the parking lot of a small business, leading her around to the back side of the building. Across the way she could see the rear portion of the police station. There was a small parking lot along the left side of the structure with a couple of squads parked there, but most of the parking was located in front of the building.

How Cooper knew how to get to the rear of the police building was a mystery. As they approached, she stumbled to a stop when she saw someone standing behind one of the trees that wasn't far from the building but also several yards away from the parking spaces that held several squads.

"Cooper?" Her voice was barely a whisper. "Do you see him?"

He dragged her down behind some brush. "Did you get a good look at his face?"

"No, he's too far away. He might be dressed in black, but I can't say for sure."

Cooper's expression turned grim. "I can't think of a logical reason for him to be standing there, unless he's watching and waiting for someone."

"Yeah. For me." Mia swallowed hard. How was it possible for these guys to know their every move?

How long would they stake out the police station, waiting for her to show up?

CHAPTER FOUR

As much as Cooper really didn't want Mia to leave, he did not like the way these guys kept popping up everywhere they went. He could only see the one guy, but he figured the second man was stationed somewhere overlooking the opposite side of the building. It appeared they were hanging around the police station, waiting for Mia. Maybe they assumed she'd report the assault. Yet hanging out in an attempt to grab her so close to the police probably wasn't smart. How could they know when a cop might walk out of the building?

Unless they had come up with a plan to drug her in order to get her quietly away from the area. The thought sent a chill down his spine.

No way was he letting either of these men get their grubby paws on Mia.

"Is there an FBI office in town?" Mia whispered.

"No. I'm not an expert, but I've been all through Gatlinburg over the past five years, and I've never seen an FBI office. I'm sure it's too small, more likely to be in Nashville and Memphis. We'll check later, after we get out of here."

Mia didn't move for long moments, but then she took a step backward. Moving slowly and as quietly as possible, they eased away from the police station.

Cooper took a different way back through the area in order to return to his apartment. Mia followed without complaint, staying close to his side. He wanted to reassure her, but there was no denying her situation was grim. The fact that neither of the men had found them at his apartment made him believe they'd be safe there.

For now.

Once they were back inside his apartment, he locked the door and leaned against it, regarding Mia thoughtfully. Neither of them spoke for several long moments.

"Now what?" Mia asked as she sank down onto the sofa. "Should we go back later tonight? Maybe when it's dark?"

"No, I have a feeling those guys are planning to hang out there for a while. Let's find the closest FBI office." He used his phone to search. Mia came over to glance over his shoulder.

"Knoxville has one," Mia said.

"Yeah, which is good because it's only a little over an hour from here." He was glad they had a destination.

She offered a wan smile. "I don't suppose you have a car to drive me to Knoxville?"

"No, sorry." His sketches didn't bring in enough money for such a luxury. Especially one he didn't need. Walking or using his skateboard were the best ways to get around. Even in winter, which were his leanest months as far as bringing in cash from his drawing.

But looking at Mia's dejected features, he wished he could offer her the ease of being able to drive right on out of here.

"I can call and leave a message," she said slowly. "There

was something on the website urging people to call and report a crime any time, day or night."

"That works. It's Friday evening, though, and the website lists the office as closed." His blue eyes captured hers. "I'm sure they have someone monitoring incoming calls."

"I hope so." Mia pulled out her disposable phone and dialed the number. The message announced to call 911 if this was an emergency, otherwise to leave a message. "This is Mia Royce, I need help getting in touch with the US Marshals. Please call me," she rattled off the number. "Thanks."

"There, now they know you need help. In the meantime, stay the night," Cooper suggested. "I'll throw in a frozen pizza for dinner. I'm sure we'll hear from someone in the morning."

"I hope so." She drew in a deep breath. "I can't help thinking that the longer I stay here, the more likely those guys will figure out where we are."

"Mia." He crossed over and knelt beside her. "We're going to be okay. They staked out the police station because they have no idea where we are." He glanced around the dim interior of his apartment. "We'll keep the lights off and pull the drapes over the windows. You can take my bed, I'll stretch out on the sofa."

"I can't take your room," she protested.

"Better for you to stay hidden, don't you think?" He offered a smile and gently squeezed her hand. "I'll keep my art supplies out, so if anyone peeks inside, they'll assume I fell asleep working. Trust me, it wouldn't be the first time I've done that."

Her dark gaze clung to his. "Okay, thank you."

He longed to pull her into his arms for a kiss. His

promise not to take advantage of her gave him the strength to release her hand and rise to his feet. "Give me a minute to throw in the pizza. In the meantime, I'll change the bedding."

"Okay."

Living with Trent who'd been a total slob had turned Cooper into a neat freak. He liked making sure everything was put in its place, especially since the tiny apartment didn't offer much room. At some level he knew his fetish for neatness was a symptom of needing to be in control. Especially after not having any say over his living arrangements in those early years of his life, being moved from one location to the next without warning.

Most of those early days were a blur. But he remembered running away because the woman kept hitting him. Yet, after that, he'd landed with the Preacher, which had been no better. He still wasn't entirely sure why Ruth had agreed to let him have his sketchbook along with the new set of oil paints that had been part of a slew of Christmas gifts people in town had donated to the fosters. He'd known the Preacher hadn't been happy, but then again, the Preacher hadn't allowed him to use them very often either.

Too late to go back and change the past now. Besides, he didn't want to think about those five years he'd spent at the Preacher's cabin. He tossed a frozen pizza into the oven, wincing at the realization the heat would make the interior of the apartment stifling yet knowing it couldn't be helped. Then he stripped and remade his bed. The chore didn't take long, and he soon returned to the living room. He leaned against the wall and smiled at her. "Okay, dinner will be ready in ten."

"I owe you so much," Mia murmured. "More than I can ever repay."

"No, you don't. My choice to get involved, remember?" Cooper didn't want her gratitude or any sort of repayment. "I'm sorry that it's so warm in here, but the good news is that there's a small window air conditioner in the bedroom."

"All the more reason you should sleep there," Mia said.

He batted down a flash of impatience. "Are you always so argumentative?"

"Argumentative? No." Mia flushed and ran her fingers through her hair. "Although I guess I have been with you."

He chose his words carefully. "I'd like to consider us friends, Mia. Friends help each other out without asking for anything in return."

"Friends." The corner of her mouth tipped up into a sad smile. "I haven't had a true friend since going into protective custody, and that's been eighteen months now. Only the last three have been here in Gatlinburg, though. In that time, I've forgotten what it's like to have the kind of friend you could count on to help out no matter what."

He pushed away from the wall. "To be honest, it's not easy for me either. I've been on my own for a very long time. Maybe we could both use some practice in the art of friendship."

"Deal." She glanced toward his minuscule kitchen. "Smells good."

He glanced at the clock and went over to check the pizza. It wasn't ready, so he pulled out plates and silverware from the cupboard. "I don't have any sun tea, but I have a pitcher of lemonade."

"I like lemonade, it's just not my favorite." Her tone was teasing.

"It should be," he joked, lighting a candle in the center of the table. With the drapes closed over the windows, the interior of the apartment was not only hot but getting darker by the minute.

Mia joined him in the kitchen. "There you go again, acting as if your opinions are better than mine."

Her face was lovelier than ever in the candlelight, and he found himself wishing he could sketch her again. Ridiculous, as he'd already sketched her twice. Three times, if you counted the drawing he'd started on the sidewalk.

About time he pulled himself together. This weird fascination with Mia wasn't healthy. She wouldn't be here for long. And he shouldn't be secretly glad she was staying the night.

Logically, he knew she didn't have many options. She was only sticking around because the two men in black were watching and waiting for her. This forced togetherness wasn't real, it was a symptom of the danger that lurked outside, ready and eager to strike.

Cooper checked the pizza. The cheese was golden brown, and the sausage gave off an enticing spicy scent. After removing it from the oven, he cut it into triangle slices and set the pizza in the center of his small table.

As expected, Mia clasped her hands and bowed her head to give a blessing. He looked down at his lap as she spoke in a hushed voice. "Dear Lord, thank You for keeping us safe today and for this food we are about to eat. We ask that You continue to watch over us as we find a way to escape those who seek to cause us harm. Amen."

He lifted his head, regarding her thoughtfully. "You used the term *we* as if I were a part of your prayer."

"I did, yes." She regarded him steadily. "I know you've had a difficult time with a man who pretended to speak the word of God, but that's behind you, Cooper. The Preacher was a horrible man who lied to you about what God is really like. He lied because God loves us in spite of our sins. God sent Jesus to us in order to forgive our sins. I truly believe God is still watching over me, and He's watching over you too."

He decided not to argue, even though he didn't necessarily agree with everything she'd said. The Preacher was a horrible man who had lied to them and to those who'd entrusted him with seven foster kids.

But the rest? Nah, he wasn't buying it. But he respected her right to believe what she wanted. "We should eat before the pizza gets cold." He rose, put a slice of pizza on her plate, then added one to his own.

It made him smile when Mia used a fork and a knife to cut into her slice of sausage pizza. "Yum."

"Not bad for a cheap frozen pizza." He grinned. "Sorry, it's not pepperoni."

"I wouldn't expect you to stock up on my favorites since you didn't even know what I liked until today."

"Next time." The words came out before he could stop them.

Her expression turned grim. "There won't be a next time, Cooper. I need to find a way to get to Knoxville in the morning. I know they don't officially open until Monday, but I would like to be close by."

"I know. I'll see what I can do to arrange that." He had friends who owned cars. Female friends. Like Rachel, who likely wouldn't be thrilled to help him relocate Mia.

Should he call Trent? He hadn't spoken to his foster brother in over a year. And that conversation had been brief as Trent had slurred his words as if he'd been drinking or on drugs. Cooper wasn't sure if his brother had even remembered the call since he hadn't heard from Trent since.

"I noticed you don't have a computer," Mia said.

"No. I don't pay for internet services here. I either use my phone, sparingly, or use the free internet at the coffee shops in town." He frowned. "What do you need?"

"Nothing." She waved a hand. "It's not a big deal."

He didn't like disappointing her, but he couldn't help the frugal way he lived. Spending money on luxuries wasn't in his nature.

For her sake, he wished he had splurged.

Maybe he was cheap at heart, at least as far as his own needs were concerned.

But for Mia? He'd spend whatever was necessary to make her happy and, more importantly, to keep her safe.

MIA THOUGHT about the fact that she'd be leaving in the morning and wished there was a way to get through Cooper's wall of resistance regarding his faith.

It would be a way to pay him back for his kindness, not that he expected anything in return.

She finished her pizza, eyeing him across the candlelight. He was incredibly attractive, especially his piercing blue eyes, yet he didn't act as if he was super aware of his looks. At least, not in the arrogant way some of the guys were in college.

His nontraditional upbringing may be partially responsible for his lack of conceit. Yet he knew women found him attractive, after all, he'd mentioned knowing Rachel wanted something more from him than simple friendship.

Not to mention, he earned his living by catering to the tourist crowd, sketching their likeness for a fee. She could easily imagine how his handsome features, arresting blue eyes, and boyish charm would bring in the tourists.

"Hey, don't worry. If we don't hear from the Feds right away, I'll find a way to get you to Knoxville." Cooper's statement punctured her thoughts.

"If all else fails, I can grab a taxi." She saw them occasionally when she passed the trolley station on her way home from work.

Cooper frowned. "Not sure that's a good idea. If I were one of those guys trying to get to you, I'd keep an eye on the trolley station where the cab drivers tend to hang out."

"They can't watch the police station and the main trolley terminal at the same time."

"You don't think so?" Cooper lifted a brow. "What if there are more than just two of them?"

The pizza sank like a rock to the bottom of her stomach. "I . . . guess I don't know for sure how many of them are out there." Frankie Germaine could very well have an endless supply of men who'd do whatever was necessary if the price was right. She wished she knew exactly what he looked like and had thought doing a computer search might help. Frankie hadn't shown up during his father's trial.

Maybe she was wrong about these guys being Frankie's men. Although she didn't know who else would want to hurt her.

"Mia, please, trust me, okay?" Cooper reached across the table to take her hand. "I'll find a way to get you out of town without anyone following."

She swallowed hard and nodded. "Okay."

"Great." He squeezed her fingers, then released her. "Are you sure you don't want more pizza?"

"Positive." Her throat was too constricted to take another bite.

Cooper took and ate the last slice. Mia rose and carried her dishes to the kitchen counter. To give herself something to do, she filled the sink with warm water, found the dish soap, and began to wash their dishes.

"I can do that," he protested.

"Don't be silly." She reached over his shoulder to take his empty plate. "I need to do something or I'll go crazy."

"What would you normally do?" Cooper finished his lemonade and brought her the empty glass.

"Practice singing, watch television, read a book." She shrugged. "Nothing exciting."

"You sing?"

She flushed. "Not the way you're imagining. I used to sing in the church choir. Before . . ." She stopped abruptly. What was wrong with her? What was it about Cooper that made her long to confide in him?

This blabbing about herself had to stop. She needed to keep her mouth shut. Her life before Gatlinburg was over. Done. Finished.

This was her new life. She worked as an administrative assistant, even though secretarial skills weren't necessarily her strong suit. She was learning though and hadn't made any big mistakes in the past few weeks.

Unless you counted not showing up for work today. Or ever again.

Mia tried not to worry about her job. It wasn't as if she needed the company to provide her with references. The US Marshals would help her obtain a new position in whatever city and state they relocated her to.

A place where she'd start all over again, a stranger in a strange land. Gatlinburg had been a huge change from Chicago, and she had no doubt that her next place would be just as much of a culture shock.

One step at a time. First she needed to escape Frankie

Germaine's men, then talk to the Feds who would connect her with the US Marshals.

And Sean? Her stomach knotted painfully. She was very much afraid something bad had happened to Deputy Marshal Sean McCarthy.

She couldn't think of any other reason that he wouldn't have responded to her call.

"Would you sing for me?"

Cooper's question caused the glass to slip from her fingers, hitting the soapy water with a splash. Thankfully, it didn't break. She glanced at him. "I don't think so. As I said, I sang in a choir, as in with other people. I'm not a soloist."

"You could let me be the judge of that." Cooper picked up a towel and dried the dishes she'd left draining in the sink.

"No, I really couldn't." Just the thought of singing for him filled her with stage fright. "Honestly, you wouldn't be interested in Christian music."

A flash of emotion darkened his eyes. "Hard to say, since I've never heard any Christian music. The Preacher ranted and raved, there was never any singing."

"That's so sad." The words popped out of her mouth before she could think about it. "Music is a wonderful way to honor God."

There was a moment of silence before Cooper said, "Trent, one of my foster brothers, was big into music. He joined a group called the Jimmy Woodrow Band and left for Nashville three years ago. He has a lot of talent."

"Sounds like you miss him."

Cooper concentrated on drying the glass in his hands as if the task was of monumental importance. "I do. But I'm happy here in Gatlinburg, the tourist business is great."

She wanted to mention art school again but decided

against bringing up a sore subject. "You don't think there are as many tourists in Nashville?"

"Oh, I'm sure there are, but the city is too big for a small-time sidewalk artist like me." He stored the glass in the cupboard. "Gatlinburg is cozy. The tourists do a lot more walking around the downtown area compared to Nashville."

"That makes sense." She couldn't help thinking that Cooper was afraid to leave the city, reluctant to try something new, like applying to art school. Likely a result of his chaotic upbringing.

In a way, she could relate. She'd been forced to leave Chicago after nearly being killed by Frank Germaine Senior and the cop on his payroll. And she was in the same situation now. She needed to leave Gatlinburg in order to survive.

The difference being that she didn't have a choice. It was leave or die.

Cooper had a choice. He was young, handsome, and talented. He could go anywhere, do whatever he wanted without worrying about staying alive. She honestly believed Cooper could do so much better for himself.

Then again, who was she to decide what made him happy?

"Well, if you don't mind, I'm going to bed early." She drained the sink and dried her hands on the towel. "It's been a long day, and the stress of being on the run has worn me out."

"I understand." Cooper stepped back from the sink, offering a small smile that didn't quite reach his eyes. "I have some calls to make anyway."

She frowned. "What kind of calls?"

He looked puzzled. "I told you I'd find a way for you to

get out of town. I have a few friends, hopefully one of them will let me borrow their car."

"Oh, okay." She was embarrassed at the flash of suspicion. "Sorry, I guess I'm still on edge. Hopefully, the FBI will call me back and arrange for someone to get me."

"Probably. But it's good to have a backup plan." He turned to head into the living room. "You can listen in if you'd like."

Mia knew she was being ridiculous. She wouldn't even be here at all if not for his quick thinking and his uncanny ability to move through the city while staying hidden from view. "No need. I trust you, Cooper."

"I hope you know I'd never do anything to hurt you." His blue gaze was intense.

"I do." She waved a hand. "I'm just overtired and feeling anxious. It never occurred to me that I'd lose my connection with Marshal Sean. It's very unnerving to feel like I'm all alone."

"You're not alone." He rested his hand on her arm. "I'm here with you. And the FBI will call soon. If not, I'll find a way to get you out of the city."

She believed him. Acting on impulse, she lifted up onto her tiptoes to kiss his cheek, only her aim was off and she ended up kissing his mouth. She flushed with embarrassment and quickly turned away. "Thanks, Cooper."

"You're welcome." His low, gravelly voice sent ripples of awareness skipping down her spine.

Oh boy. Time to put some distance between them. She turned and sought refuge in the bathroom. To use the facilities, but more so to get herself under some semblance of control.

Kissing Cooper had been a mistake. Not because she hadn't enjoyed it, but because it made her want more.

So much more.

Mia splashed cold water on her face, then went into Cooper's bedroom. He'd changed the sheets, but the entire space still smelled like him. It was a scent she'd have loved to bottle up to take with her.

"Mia?" Cooper rapped softly on the door.

Steeling her resolve, she crossed over to open it. "Yes?"

"I—uh, have plenty of T-shirts. You're welcome to sleep in one." He looked a bit embarrassed at mentioning her sleepwear.

"Thanks." She stepped aside, giving him room to enter. He opened the second dresser drawer and gestured to the neatly folded stack of T-shirts. "Take whatever you need."

"Okay. Did you make your calls?"

He nodded and walked toward the door. "I left a couple of messages. I'm sure I'll hear back soon." He glanced at her over his shoulder. "Good night, Mia."

"Good night."

He left, closing the door behind him. She plugged in her phone, then chose a bright yellow shirt from the pile. Of course it smelled like Cooper, but somehow, the musky scent helped her relax.

A low agonizing cry woke Mia from a sound sleep. She froze, her heart pounding as she tried to place the sound. Had it come from outside? Was someone being mugged right outside the window?

She heard it again, a low moan followed by the words, "Stop, please stop!"

Cooper! She bolted out of bed, yanked the door open, and hurried into the living room. Cooper was lying on the sofa, his head moving from side to side as if dodging blows.

Tiptoeing around the scattered art supplies, she put a

hand on his shoulder. "Cooper, wake up. You're having a bad dream."

"No, please," he moaned again.

She couldn't stand to see him like this. She shook his shoulder with more vigor. "Cooper, wake up!"

His eyes popped open, but he stared at something off in the darkness. She swallowed hard, glancing over her shoulder to verify nothing was back there. Was he still asleep? Was he about to sleepwalk? Did he do this often?

Then the moment was gone as he turned to look at her. "Mia? What's wrong? Are you okay?"

"Me?" She managed a strangled laugh. "I'm fine. You're the one having a nightmare."

His gaze clouded, and he glanced away. "Sorry about that."

She knelt beside him. "Don't apologize. Not about having a nightmare. I've had my share of them since the night . . ." Her voice trailed off.

Cooper dragged his hand through his hair and sat up. "It's been a long time since I dreamed about the Preacher."

"I'm sure the memories resurfaced because we've been running away from bad guys." She put her hand on his knee. "My fault, really."

"Not at all your fault." He gently cupped her cheek. "Thanks for being here with me."

She leaned forward at the same time that he lowered his head to hers. His kiss was sweet, gentle at first, but morphed into something more.

Mia threaded her fingers through his hair, reveling in the heat and possessiveness of his kiss.

Desperately wishing for something she couldn't have.

CHAPTER FIVE

Cooper lost his ability to think the moment his mouth fused with Mia's, her sweet taste filling his mind with desire. He'd never experienced this instant internal combustion during a mere kiss, and the intensity shook him to his core.

No woman had ever had this much power over him, and it was a bit scary. In some deep recess of his brain, Cooper knew he'd do anything for this woman in his arms, despite the fact that he barely knew her.

He didn't want to let her go, but somehow he found the strength to end their kiss, lowering his forehead to rest against hers. "I, uh, should apologize." His voice was hoarse, and he tried not to sound as pathetic as he felt. "I promised not to take advantage of you."

To his surprise, Mia chuckled softly. She lifted her head to look him in the eye. "How do you know I didn't try to take advantage of you?"

He stared at her for a long moment, not sure what to say in response. While she'd participated in the kiss as much as he had, he was far more street savvy than she was. The air of fragile innocence that clung to her made him choose his words carefully. "I'd love nothing more than to kiss you again, Mia. But we both know starting something, trying to have a relationship, won't lead anywhere. Tomorrow morning . . ." His throat tightened, making it impossible to finish his thought.

She'd be gone.

All mirth faded from her features, making him feel as bad as if he'd kicked a puppy. "You're right."

"Mia, if things were different . . ." Again, he couldn't seem to find the words to express his feelings. He was lousy at this kind of thing. He was much better at expressing himself through his art.

"Yes, well, if things were different, we wouldn't have met at all, right?" The corner of her mouth tipped up in a sad smile. "I'd barely heard of Gatlinburg, Tennessee. Hadn't ever had the city on my list of places to visit before I was—ah—brought here. And even though I noticed you sketching on the sidewalk, I never would have approached you."

"You wouldn't?" That took him by surprise.

"No, you were out of my league."

"You've got that completely backwards. You're out of my league." He gazed into her heart-shaped face, her dark brown eyes, trying to commit every detail to memory.

"You flatter me, but I know the truth." She waved a hand. "I'm just saying my unique situation is the only reason we've met at all. That and your keen observation that noticed the man following me."

"I guess you're right about that." He couldn't imagine why a witness would be located to a small city like Gatlinburg, but maybe the remoteness of the place and its proximity to the Smoky Mountains had made it seem like a good place to hide.

Hadn't he chosen to stick around in Gatlinburg rather than to follow Trent? Sure, his tourism business was better here, but deep down he'd also wanted to be close to the Smoky Mountains just in case he needed to disappear again.

Why? He had no clue. As some sort of security blanket? Probably.

"I should get some sleep." Mia rose to her feet. He missed her warmth, her honeysuckle fragrance, the moment she moved away.

He had to curl his fingers into his palms to hold himself back from reaching for her again. "Thanks for waking me up." The nightmare that had brought Mia out of the bedroom was now nothing but a distant memory. The impact of their kiss had taken over, leaving no room for anything else.

"You're welcome." Mia flashed a smile. "Good night."

"Good night." He watched as she disappeared into his bedroom. Stretching out on the sofa, he placed his hand over his heart in a vain effort to stop his racing pulse. It was three in the morning, and he felt certain he wouldn't be able to fall back asleep. Staring up at the ceiling, he told himself not to get emotionally attached to Mia. Their time together would be short, just long enough for her to get out of the city.

Yet he knew he'd never forget her.

He dozed on and off until about five o'clock. He tiptoed into the kitchen to make coffee, then picked up his sketch pad.

As usual, he felt compelled to draw Mia, but this time, he thought it might be better for him to draw the two men who'd tried to grab her. If nothing else, he could turn them over to the FBI agents.

Spurred by the idea of helping, he sketched quickly, doing his best to remember the brief image of the first man he'd kicked in the groin. Cooper had mostly seen the guy from the back, with only the barest glimpse of his surprised face before he'd bent over in pain.

He drew with such intensity his fingers cramped. He paused to shake them out, then belatedly remembered the coffee. He set the sketch aside and went into the kitchen. To his surprise, he found Mia standing there, her dark hair adorably messy from sleep.

The urge to kiss her right then and there was overwhelming.

"Good morning," she murmured while reaching for a mug from the cupboard. "I hope you were able to fall back asleep."

"I'm okay." He didn't want to admit that thoughts of Mia had made sleeping impossible. "You look great."

She rolled her eyes and poured herself coffee. "The just rolled out of bed look is in these days."

It was, actually, so that made him laugh. "You'll find milk in the fridge, sugar in the cupboard."

"Thanks." She doctored her coffee before taking a sip. "No call back yet from Sean or the FBI. Maybe because it's a Saturday? Did you find a ride?"

"Um, let me check." He winced at the flash of guilt. "Sorry, I've been sketching, so I haven't looked at my phone."

"What are you sketching?" She looked truly interested.

He poured himself coffee and led the way into the living room. "I'm sketching the two men who tried to grab you. I thought it might help the FBI to identify them."

Mia nodded slowly, setting her coffee aside to look

closely at the sketch. "This looks just like the first guy who was following me."

"Thanks, that was the goal." He reached for the sketchbook. "I need to do the second guy yet."

"The one you punched in the face." Mia glanced at his bruised and swollen knuckles. "Are you going to sketch his face the way it looked before the punch or after?"

He chuckled. "Before, as I'm hoping he and the other guy are both well-known criminals with mug shots on file."

"Wow, this is incredible. You could do this for a living, Cooper."

He frowned. "I do sketch for a living."

"Oh yes, of course." Her face flushed beet red. "That came out wrong. I just meant you could probably find work as a police sketch artist if that was something you were interested in doing."

There was no reason to be wounded by her comment, although it was pretty obvious Mia didn't consider street art as a viable career choice. "It's not the same thing," he pointed out in a gruff tone. "A police sketch artist pulls details from a witness and sketches the image based on what that person says. That's not a skill I possess. I'm drawing these guys by memory."

"Oh, I guess I hadn't considered that angle." Mia kept her gaze focused on the sketch as if unable to meet his gaze. "It's just that you're so good, Cooper."

Good but not living up to his potential? He told himself to shake it off. He wasn't interested in attending an art school or anything structured like that. He needed to be free and was happy sketching for a living. Mia's opinion shouldn't matter this much, especially since she was leaving. He crossed over to take his phone off the charger, glancing down at the screen. No text messages or missed calls. Hmm. He found it odd that neither Suzy nor Chloe had responded to his request to borrow their car for the day. He hoped that wasn't a bad sign.

He could try Rachel, letting her know that he was using the car to drop Mia off in another city. Maybe she'd agree once she knew the end result would mean that Mia wouldn't be in Gatlinburg any longer.

Or maybe Rachel would simply tell him to jump into the Tennessee River.

Women. Why did they have to make life so complicated?

"What's wrong?"

He glanced at Mia, belatedly realizing he was scowling at his phone. "Nothing, it's probably too early to hear back from my friends."

"Or they're not willing to let you borrow a car."

He shrugged and glanced at the time. "It's barely seven o'clock. We'll give them some time before I start bugging them. And who knows, maybe the FBI office will call back soon as well. I need to do a second sketch anyway."

"I'll cook breakfast," Mia offered.

He waved toward the kitchen. "Help yourself. Not a lot of options, sorry. I tend to eat out more than I eat in."

"I saw a carton of eggs, that should be good enough." Mia took her coffee into the kitchen, leaving him alone with his sketchbook and his turbulent thoughts.

He flipped the page on his sketchbook and began to draw the second man. The two men had both worn black clothing and a black baseball cap, but their faces had been very different. The guy he'd punched had Nordic features, straight short blond hair, a thin nose, and light green eyes, while the first guy had sported a more rugged look, including a fine scar above his right eyebrow. The Nordic guy hadn't had any distinguishing marks or tattoos, but that didn't stop Cooper from spending time on every detail of his face that he could remember.

The tantalizing scent of eggs and toast made his stomach grumble. He put the finishing touches on the second sketch and carefully pulled it off the pad. He propped both sketches up against the back of the sofa, eyeing them critically.

They were decent replicas of the two men who'd tried to hurt Mia, but Cooper wasn't convinced they'd be enough for the Feds to recognize them. Partially because the base-ball caps had hidden details about the shape of their heads, the texture of their hair.

A name, a fingerprint, some other unique feature would go a long way to finding out who these guys were. But Cooper figured the two sketches were better than nothing.

"Breakfast is ready," Mia called.

He carried his now empty coffee mug into the kitchen and gaped in surprise at the plates she'd set on the table. "You made omelets?"

"You had some veggies in there, and cheese, so it seemed like a good idea." She frowned. "Why, don't you like veggie omelets?"

"I love them, and this looks amazing." He would normally have just tossed the eggs into a pan, scrambled them up, and ate them on a piece of toast. "Thanks."

"It's the least I can do." She filled his mug and hers before dropping into the chair across from him. He knew she'd want to pray, so he folded his hands in his lap, bowed his head, and waited. "Dear Lord, we thank You for this food we are about to eat. We also ask that You bless us and guide us safely away from those who seek us harm. Amen."

Amen.

The response flashed in his mind, catching him off guard before he could stop it. He glanced at Mia, relieved he hadn't said the word out loud. He cleared his throat and said, "That was nice."

Her smile lit up her entire face, making him feel guilty for not participating more. Which was crazy since he'd never prayed in his life and had no intention of starting now.

Except he kinda had just by listening to her prayer.

He was halfway through his omelet when his phone rang. Cooper jumped up and hurried into the living room to answer. "Hello?"

"Coop? It's Suzy."

"Hey, thanks for calling me back." He walked back into the kitchen, holding the phone to his ear. "I need a huge favor."

"I heard," Suzy said wryly. "You want to borrow my car."

"I do, yes." His gaze locked on Mia's. "Will you let me use it for the day? I promise to return it with a full tank of gas."

"Yeah, that's fine." She didn't sound entirely convinced. "Where are you headed?"

"Knoxville."

"What's in Knoxville?"

The question threw him off for a moment. "Art supplies," he finally said. "They have a better selection there, and I don't want to waste money on a taxi. You know how it is in tourist season, gotta strike while the iron is hot."

"Does this mean you'll do a sketch for me when you return?" Suzy's tone was teasing.

"Of course." He liked Suzy, but he wasn't interested in anything more. Promising a sketch was no hardship, although he suspected Suzy really wanted something more personal. Her sketch would likely come with a price, like a dinner date. "Can I pick up the keys?"

"Give me an hour or so," Suzy said. "I'll drive to work, and you can meet me at the hotel." It wasn't a suggestive comment, Suzy worked in the restaurant of one of the large hotels in Gatlinburg. She claimed the tips were phenomenal and had offered to get him a job there on several occasions.

Cooper had done plenty of restaurant work, among other odd jobs, until his sketching had seemed to catch on with the tourists. He wasn't interested in going back to the restaurant business, then again, he wasn't going to close the door on the possibility either. He gave Mia a thumbs-up. "That's perfect, Suzy. Thanks so much. See you in an hour."

"Looking forward to it," Suzy said before ending the call.

He set the phone down and resumed eating his breakfast. "We're set. If the FBI calls, we can always arrange to meet them someplace halfway."

She nodded, her dark gaze full of relief. "Okay, great. Thanks." She stood and carried her plate to the sink. "I'm going to take a shower if you don't mind."

"Help yourself." His omelet had grown cold, but he wasn't one to waste food, so he finished every bite, along with the toast. He was deeply grateful Suzy had come through for him without his having to beg. Yet the news also caused a small knot to form in his stomach.

He only had a short amount of time to spend with Mia.

A few measly hours before she walked out of his life, forever.

MIA TRIED to ignore the stark sense of desolation that washed over her. She took a shower, grimacing when she had to put on the same clothing she'd worn the day before. She took advantage of washing her hair because she had no idea how long it would take for the FBI to return her call. And maybe they were already trying to contact the US Marshals Service so one of their deputies could relocate her to yet another new and allegedly safe place.

But more importantly, she needed a moment to herself. To find a way to rein in her chaotic emotions.

She didn't know Cooper very well, but he'd become her lifeline in a very short period of time. Leaving him to go with strangers wouldn't be easy, but it was necessary.

Hadn't she placed him in enough danger already? She was worried that even once she was safely out of Gatlinburg, the two men would find Cooper and kill him simply because he'd prevented them from getting to her.

Something she wanted to ask the FBI about, once they returned her call.

And who was this Suzy who was so easily handing Cooper her car keys? Cooper had claimed not to have a girlfriend, but it was clear that several of the women in the area would love the opportunity to change his mind.

Including her.

Yeah, that was so not happening.

Enough. Mia gave herself a mental shake as she dragged Cooper's comb through her wet dark hair. This weird dependence she had on Cooper wasn't healthy. Granted, that explosive kiss they'd shared didn't help matters. Especially when she'd wanted to throw herself into his arms and kiss him again first thing this morning.

Yep, she was losing her mind. She had much bigger issues to deal with. Instead of thinking about kissing Cooper, she needed to remain focused on the dangerous men who'd followed her and gone as far as to stake out the police station in town in an effort to kidnap her.

To kill her.

Cooper's sketches of the two men had sent chills down her spine. She had no doubt they were a couple of thugs hired by Frankie Germaine, but of course, she couldn't prove that. The blond guy who'd grabbed her, letting go only when Cooper had punched him in the face, had only said three words.

I've got you.

Had there been a trace of an accent in his voice? Or was she imagining it based on Cooper's artful drawing? The man looked as if he'd come from Norway, or maybe Sweden. Yet that didn't really make sense since Frank Germaine Senior was of Italian descent and had resided in Chicago. Although she really had no idea where Frankie Germaine Junior lived.

Whatever. It wasn't her job to worry about arresting Frankie Germaine. That was the role of the FBI, or maybe even the US Marshals. Surely one agency or the other would be able to bring him to justice.

What worried her more was Deputy Sean McCarthy. A full twenty-four hours had gone by without hearing from him. That just didn't seem right, not in an emergency after being attacked. And while she'd prayed for God to keep him safe, deep down, she feared the deputy was dead.

Likely murdered by Frankie's men.

A ripple of goosebumps rose on her skin. Mia took a deep breath and did her best to stay focused. There was nothing she could do for Sean other than getting to the closest FBI office and waiting for them to return her call. Personally, she'd be glad to get out of Gatlinburg. Thanks to Cooper's friend Suzy allowing them to borrow her car, they'd be on the road within the hour.

If only she'd have called the FBI officer earlier. At the time, it seemed logical to wait for Sean to call her back. Unfortunately, it was too late to go back and second-guess her decisions.

"Mia? Are you finished?"

She spun toward Cooper's voice. "Oh, yes. Sorry. The bedroom and bathroom are all yours."

"Thanks." His smile didn't quite reach his eyes.

She edged past him, the small apartment seemingly more crowded than ever. She sat in the living room near the window, hoping the sun heating up the interior of the room would also help dry her hair.

It took her a moment to realize her quest was solely so she would look her best when she met Cooper's friend Suzy. As if they were rivals fighting for Cooper's attention.

Ridiculous. Suzy lived here in town while Mia would soon be relocated to another part of the country. She glanced around the apartment. It wouldn't be easy to leave the one place she'd felt safe.

Fifteen minutes later, Cooper joined her. His hair was wet too, but he looked good regardless. She sent him a few glances as he packed his art supplies into his large knapsack, including his two sketches of the men who'd tried to grab her. If she had one iota of talent, she'd sketch him, but she had to settle for committing his image to memory.

When he tossed the pack over his shoulder, she furrowed her brow. "Are you planning to work in Knoxville?"

"Huh?" He glanced at her in surprise, then smiled

sheepishly. "Probably not, but I don't go anywhere without my art supplies."

"Okay, then." She double-checked her purse to make sure she had her phone and charger cord. "Lead the way."

He looked at her for a long moment before pulling out his keys. He opened the door and glanced up and down the hallway before gesturing for her to join him.

Mia didn't say anything as Cooper once again led her out the rear door of the small apartment building. The pungent scent from the dumpster made her wrinkle her nose and breathe through her mouth, but Cooper didn't seem to notice. He captured her hand and led her past several streets that looked vaguely familiar from yesterday.

Since being relocated here, she hadn't spent much time in the tourist section of Gatlinburg. The business she worked at was located on the other side of the city as was her apartment. For those first few weeks she'd focused mostly on doing a good job, despite her lack of administrative skills. She'd ordered books online and spent her free time reading. It was only when she'd longed for the sanctuary of church that she'd broached this area.

A decision that had proven detrimental to her well-being.

Yet one she couldn't regret since the end result was that she'd met Cooper.

Taking his zigzag pattern added a little extra time to their journey. It was just over an hour when they reached the large hotel where Suzy apparently worked. Cooper glanced around, but then led the way inside.

"Wow, this place is busy," she whispered as they entered the air-conditioned and chaotic lobby. People with luggage were checking in and leaving, some of the kids were running around in swimsuits and flip-flops.

"It's one of the nicer hotels, complete with a water park," Cooper told her. "This way."

He headed down a hallway toward a large restaurant with a scenic view overlooking the Smoky Mountains. Cooper raised his hand, flagging down a slender woman with honey-blond hair pulled back from her face.

"Hey, Coop." Suzy frowned when she saw Mia. "I thought you were going to Knoxville for art supplies?"

"I am, but Mia needs a ride too, she lives in Knoxville." The lies fell easily from his lips, and she couldn't help thinking he must have had a lot of practice with the art of deception. "I really appreciate you letting me use your wheels, Suzy. Thanks so much."

Suzy dropped her car keys into his outstretched hand. "Sure, no problem. Will you swing by later when you get back? We can grab a bite to eat while I'm on break."

"Sure thing." Cooper flashed his amazing smile. "I'm sure this trip won't take long."

"It's nice to meet you, Suzy," Mia said. "Thanks for allowing me to ride along with Cooper."

"No problem." The woman's tone was casual, but her gaze was narrow. Mia felt certain that if Cooper had asked to borrow the car on Mia's behalf, the answer would have been a straight-out no.

"Where are you parked?" Cooper asked.

"Along the furthest edge of the parking lot." Suzy shrugged. "Where the employees are required to park."

"Okay, thanks again." Cooper bent over to give Suzy a quick kiss on the cheek, which erased most of the annoyance in her features. "Later."

"Can't wait." Suzy smiled before turning away to return to her duties.

"Wow, you're quite the lady killer, aren't you?" Mia

glanced at him as they threaded their way back through the congested lobby.

"I'm not," he denied quickly. "I can't help it if some women are drawn to artists."

"Ha ha, good one."

He shot her an exasperated look. "I had to be nice to her, or we wouldn't have a vehicle to get you out of here. It's not like I want to have lunch or dinner with her."

"Poor baby, I can tell you're suffering." She'd meant to tease him, but deep down, she felt a pang of jealously.

Probably the same feeling Suzy felt toward her.

Outside, the August heat and humidity was a slap in the face after being inside the air-conditioned hotel. Cooper led the way around to the side of the building where the parking lot was located.

"What kind of car are we looking for?" she asked as they walked past rows and rows of vehicles. Clearly Gatlinburg was a destination that tourists traveled to by car.

"An old Chevy Lumina." He craned his neck and gestured. "I see it. It's silver, with a liberal amount of rust."

Minutes later, they were inside Suzy's car. They both rolled down their windows as Cooper backed up and turned the car toward the main highway.

"Whew, it's a steamy one." She played with the controls. "I'm not sure the air works."

"Yeah, it probably doesn't," Cooper agreed. "But we'll be out of town on the interstate soon enough."

Time to stop complaining. She leaned back in her seat, watching the gaggle of tourists milling about. It occurred to her that Cooper had not only cut his sketching short yesterday but that he'd likely miss a good portion of today too.

All because of her.

"I wish I could repay you for what you've done for me."

Cooper didn't answer, and when she looked over at him, his gaze went between the windshield and the rearview mirror.

Mia turned in her seat, glancing back through the window. "What's wrong?"

"There's a black truck back with tinted windows that seems to be following us." His expression was grim, his fingers tight on the steering wheel.

"But . . . how could they have tracked us down?" She grasped the arm rest as Cooper took an abrupt right turn.

"I don't know." He drove a short way down the street, then cut through a parking lot. Mia glanced over her shoulder, horrified to realize the black truck with tinted windows was still there, following close behind.

Frankie Germaine's men had found them!

CHAPTER SIX

Cooper battled a wave of desperate fear as he drove as fast as he dared through the tourist crowded city. He was far better at evading people on foot—driving was not something he did very often, and never with bad guys chasing him.

What if he caused Mia to be captured and killed? His stomach knotted so tightly he almost cried out in pain.

He'd never be able to live with himself.

"They're still following." Mia's low agonizing tone only made him feel worse. "How did they find us?"

"Are they tracking your phone?"

"It's only a basic prepaid one." Still, she opened her window and tossed it out.

Cooper kept an eye on the truck while trying to come up with an escape plan. He considered driving straight to the police station, but he worried the men in the truck had that possibility covered. He couldn't afford to ignore the fact that they may have brought in reinforcements.

He drove the car down a narrow alley, then turned left and then right, doing his best to lose the black truck with its tinted windows. But his maneuvers didn't work as well as he'd hoped, the slower speeds making it easy enough for the truck to keep pace.

Cranking the wheel hard to the left, he went up and over a curb to cut through a grocery store parking lot. On the other side, he took another right-hand turn, then another, searching for the winding road that would take them out of the city.

"Where are we going?" Mia asked as he hit the gas.

"Trying to lose them." He didn't take his eyes off the road before them. He thought if they could get far enough ahead of the black truck, they'd have a better chance of losing them.

Maybe.

"They're still back there, but not as close as before." Mia was turned in her seat, watching through their rear window. "Keep going, Cooper. We can do this."

He appreciated her faith in his abilities. The country road twisted and curved, which was good in that they were able to stay well ahead of the truck. Now he just needed a place to turn off the road so they could evade the men behind them once and for all.

Easier said than done.

"Look for a road that will take us off this highway." He shot a quick glance at her. "I hate to tell you I'm not as familiar with the highways outside of the city."

"Okay." She offered a tremulous smile. "We're going to get away, Cooper. God is watching over us."

Now wasn't the time to argue over faith. He continued to scan the road ahead, hoping there was a turnoff within the next few miles.

"There!" Mia pointed excitedly to a spot on her side of the highway. "I think that's a road."

He craned his neck in an effort to see better. The thick

trees and brush lining the road made it difficult to pinpoint the location. "I hope it's not a private driveway, or we'll be exchanging one problem for another."

A blinking red light on the instrument panel caught his attention. Uh-oh. That couldn't be good. He eyed the gas gauge, they had less than a quarter tank left. But he didn't think that was the problem. The light was shaped like an engine, and while he didn't know much about the inner workings of a combustible engine, he felt certain the blinking light was bad news.

Had they run out of oil? Or was there a lack of coolant in the radiator? Or something else?

A quick glance at the rearview mirror showed nothing but empty highway behind them. He hit the brake and turned into the deeply rutted road.

Was it his imagination or was the light blinking faster? What if the car engine blew up?

"What's wrong?" Mia must have noted his grim expression.

"The engine light is on." Through the trees, he could see a house, more of a cabin really, sitting on the hill.

There was no sign of anyone being home, but that didn't mean someone wasn't inside, watching their every move. When they'd escaped from the Preacher's cabin, he, Trent, and Sawyer had come across some hill people who greeted them with fully loaded shotguns rather than a friendly smile. This cabin wasn't anything fancy, so he feared this might be one of those types of residences.

Not good.

Cooper stopped the car and cut the engine. There was a strange clicking sound for several long moments before the vehicle went silent. He had a bad feeling the car wouldn't start up again without mechanical help of some kind.

Suzy was going to kill him.

If the men in the black truck didn't find them and kill them first.

"Come on, we'll need to walk from here." He pushed open his car door and slid out from behind the wheel.

"Walk where?" Mia followed suit, watching in surprise as he lifted out his knapsack and looped the straps over his shoulders. "Why not go up to the cabin, see if anyone there can help? Maybe we can call the police."

"First, we need some distance from the car." He was operating on gut instinct now, those same instincts that had kept him alive over the past thirteen years. "We'll watch the cabin for a while, see if anyone comes out."

Mia didn't look convinced but readily followed his lead. He moved quickly and silently, picking a careful path through the thick brush. In a flash, Cooper's mind took him back to the woods of North Carolina, where he, Trent, and Sawyer had hidden and watched as firefighters battled the blaze that engulfed the Preacher's cabin.

The thick smoke had prevented them from being seen. And they hadn't lingered for long. Being a year older, Sawyer had taken the role of leader, taking them farther and farther away from the burning cabin. Not just to avoid being sent back into the system, but in case the woods around them began to burn. The Smoky Mountains were famous for the mist that hovered over them, but the fire had broken out in fall, which meant there hadn't been as much rainfall to keep the fire from spreading.

"Cooper?"

He'd been so lost in the past he'd forgotten about Mia. He turned to see she was having trouble keeping up.

"Sorry." He mentally smacked himself upside the head

as he hurried back to her side. Mia hadn't lived in the woods the way he once had.

The way he'd vowed to never do again.

"Haven't we gone far enough?" She bent over at the waist, bracing her hands on her knees.

Not by a long shot. Still, she looked worn out, as if this had all been too much for her to handle. "We can rest for a few minutes." He glanced around the area. "Over here, behind this large evergreen tree."

She nodded and stumbled toward the tree he'd indicated. He covered her from the back, realizing he should have kept her ahead of him the whole time anyway.

He hadn't seen a gun on either of the two men during their brief scuffle, but that didn't mean they weren't armed.

And dangerous.

Mia collapsed onto the ground. She wrapped her arms around her bent knees and rested her forehead on them.

"I'm sorry." He felt like complete idiot for dragging her along without a thought as to her endurance. "Stay here, I'm going to check on the cabin."

That statement had her lifting her head. She pushed her hair from her face. "You're leaving me here?" There was a ragged edge of panic underlying her tone.

"Mia, relax." He rested a hand on her slender shoulder. "I know the woods can be deceiving, but trust me, we haven't gone that far. I'm only going to walk a few yards to see if I can find an area where I can see the cabin, okay?"

She covered his hand with hers, her gaze beseeching. "Don't leave me, Cooper. I've never been camping, I flunked out of the Girl Scouts."

That made him smile. "Come on, no one flunks out of scouting."

"I did," she insisted.

"I don't believe it."

"It's true. I refused to use the porta potty, and well, things went downhill from there." She looked so dejected he had to fight the urge to kiss her again. "Do you have a compass? What if you get lost?"

He'd never used a compass, had never been in the Boy Scouts for that matter. Everything he knew had been learned the hard way, through trial and error in those weeks after escaping the Preacher's cabin. They'd used the sun and the stars to keep track of which direction they were going, and by now, he knew north, south, east, and west by instinct. Even after all this time, when he'd thought he'd put this kind of thing behind him.

Focusing on his art had carried him forward, helping him to let go of the past that threatened to hold him back.

"I won't go far," he promised. "Trust me, Mia. I have plenty of experience being in the woods, lived off the land for weeks after the fire. I won't lose you."

She released his hand and expelled a loud breath. "I'll hold you to that."

He nodded and grinned. "I'm sure you will." He rose and moved out from behind the large pine tree toward the cabin they'd left in their wake.

Dropping down behind a thicket, he peered through the foliage, searching for the cabin. Made of wood, it blended well with the trees. But he also knew they hadn't gotten that far.

He took his time, searching carefully. He found the rust-covered silver Lumina first, wincing at how obvious it looked sitting in the middle of the forest. So far, though, no one had come out of the cabin to approach the vehicle. Because the cabin was empty?

Or because the occupant was hiding inside holding a weapon while waiting and watching?

After another couple of minutes, he found the cabin, farther to the right than he'd remembered. He must be losing his touch, he'd led Mia off on an angle.

He hated to admit he was out of practice. Living in an apartment and sketching tourists was the easy life compared to where he'd come from. Obviously, he needed to keep up his survival skills if he wanted to remain prepared for the worst-case scenario.

He watched for several long minutes, trying to catch a glimpse of movement from the owner of the property. They were likely trespassing, although they hadn't come across any property markers.

As the minutes ticked by in his head, Cooper decided the owners of the cabin weren't there. Yet he didn't want to stick around either. The Lumina sat in the rutted driveway like a silver beacon. He was afraid the occupants in the black truck might retrace their path and stumble across the car.

And with the engine light blinking, he didn't dare use it as a way to escape. If the engine even started, which he highly doubted.

Inwardly sighing, he decided it would be best for him and Mia to hike out of there. Once they were far enough from the Lumina and the cabin, he could call Suzy to let her know about the car and then maybe follow up with Chloe to request a ride back into town.

He hesitated, wondering again if he should call Trent in Nashville. It had been well over a year since he'd spoken to Trent. Would his foster brother even bother to come help? Cooper couldn't say for certain.

Maybe it would be better to make a call to the police.

And they'd have to call the FBI again as Mia had dumped her phone. But the police were closer. They could report how the black truck had followed them and how the two men had tried to grab Mia. They could explain about how Mia was in witness protection and needed to get into federal custody ASAP.

If the police came to them, they wouldn't have to worry about the bad guys lingering around the police station. The cops could protect them, even if the bad guys had brought in reinforcements, right?

Right.

It wasn't the best plan in the world, but it was better than nothing. And hopefully enough of one to put Mia at ease.

When he turned to make his way back to Mia, the sound of a car engine reached him. Cooper froze, carefully scanning the area without moving a muscle.

There!

The rumble of the car engine grew louder as if the vehicle was coming toward them. The owner of the cabin?

A glimpse of movement between the green foliage caught his eye. His gut clenched. Beads of sweat popped out on his forehead.

No, it couldn't be.

But it was.

The black truck moved carefully and deliberately through the trees, heading directly for the silver Lumina.

Cooper eased backward one step at a time until he reached the towering pine tree where Mia was waiting. He put a finger to his lips, indicating she needed to remain silent.

Her eyes widened in horror as she rose shakily to her feet. He tried to smile reassuringly but feared it was more of a grimace. He came up beside her and lowered his mouth to her ear. "The black truck found the Lumina."

She gasped, then covered her mouth with her hand. She began to tremble, but there wasn't time for her to fall apart.

"Stay strong, Mia. We need to move as quietly as possible," he murmured softly. "I need you to go first so I can cover you from behind."

She shook her head. "You first," she whispered. "It's easier for me to follow in your footsteps."

He didn't like it, but there wasn't time to argue either. And she was right, he was better suited to navigate silently through the woods. "Okay, let's go."

She lightly grasped his knapsack as he led the way through the woods. He chose the easiest and hopefully the quietest path he could find.

As they moved through the woods with excruciating slowness, he wanted to tell Mia that if God was real and He truly cared about her safety, now would be a good time to pray.

Unfortunately, God had never been there for him. And there was no reason for Cooper to think that had changed one little bit.

MIA CONCENTRATED on stepping in the exact same place Cooper did, although she winced with every small sound they made. It was difficult to wrap her mind around the fact that the men in the truck had found their car.

Well, Suzy's car.

Cooper mentioned they hadn't gotten as far away from the cabin as she'd thought, which meant the two men could fan out and search for them.

She stumbled, barely managing to catch herself by clinging to Cooper's knapsack. She'd wanted to suggest they leave it behind but decided he probably couldn't bear to part with his art supplies. She could even understand his desire to hang on to it.

His art was his life.

A wave of desolation hit hard. She'd dragged Cooper into this mess to the point he was in just as deep as she was. Unfortunately, she knew better than most that Frankie Germaine's men wouldn't stop until they were both dead.

Mia closed her eyes and sent up a silent prayer. *Please, God, please keep us safe in Your care!*

Cooper didn't believe, but she still felt confident God would watch over both of them. After all, He had sent Cooper to protect her. God had also guided them away from the bad guys several times already. Surely, He was still watching over them.

Something crawled along the back of her neck, and she had to swallow a scream as she slapped at it. When she saw the size of the spider that had been dancing along her bare skin, she nearly fainted right then and there.

Don't. Think. About. The. Bugs.

The silent mantra didn't work. After seeing the spider, she was hyperaware of every buzzing mosquito, every fly, even the tiny little gnats that whipped past her line of vision. The woods were teaming with insects, and likely other wildlife as well. Mia knew she was being ridiculous and that the men in the black truck were far more dangerous than the bugs living in the woods around them, but she couldn't help herself. If she'd had bug spray in her purse, she'd have gladly used every drop.

She'd never been a tomboy. Had never camped and had absolutely refused to use the porta potty at day camp. She'd called her stepmother, begging to come home, and hadn't gone to the bathroom until she'd gotten there.

The Girl Scout thing had been her dad's idea, thankfully her stepmother had supported Mia's stance on using the disgusting porta potties and dealing with bugs.

It was one of the few times her stepmother had been on her side. Not that Audrey had been mean to her because the woman had done her best. But while Mia wasn't a tomboy, she wasn't a glamour girl either.

Just a plain Jane who'd loved reading, eating out, and singing in the church choir.

She gave herself a mental shake, realizing she was very close to losing the slight grip she had on her self-control. This wasn't the time to reminisce about all she'd lost. Cooper was doing his best to keep them alive.

Mia forced herself to concentrate on following Cooper's footsteps while keeping as quiet as possible.

The thundering beat of her heart and her ragged breathing were so loud, she couldn't tell if the guys in the black truck were also moving through the woods, following them.

She wanted to believe Cooper would have said something if he'd heard them coming, but then again, he may have kept the information to himself to avoid sending her into a full-blown panic attack.

A concern that wasn't too far off the mark.

Their progress was slow as they walked for what seemed like forever. Mia trusted Cooper's abilities but also knew she wouldn't last much longer. If he didn't take a break soon, she'd likely fall flat on her face, forcing the issue.

And possibly making enough noise to catch the bad guy's attention.

"Cooper," she whispered.

He didn't answer but led her over toward a trio of trees. He gestured for her to sit down and carefully shrugged the knapsack off his back. As she sank gratefully to the ground, trying not to notice the beetle crawling away from them, it occurred to her that Cooper had moved stealthily despite carrying the extra weight on his back.

The stark truth was like a slap to the face.

She was holding him back.

Mia hung her head and took several deep breaths. Not only had she put Cooper in danger, but now that they were on the run from bad guys, she was slowing him down.

"Maybe you should go on without me," she whispered.

"No." He knelt next to his knapsack and pulled out a bottle of water. "Here, take just a few sips. We'll have to ration this until we find a stream."

She gratefully sipped the water, although it was difficult to hold herself back from draining the bottle. Then his words registered. Find a stream? It wasn't safe to drink from the stream, weren't there bugs in the water?

Forget! About! The bugs!

"You doing okay?" Cooper's low voice rumbled in her ear.

She managed a nod, even though she felt like crying. Cooper was doing his best to keep her safe, the least she could do was to keep her mouth shut and avoid whining about it.

"I know this is difficult, but we need to keep moving." There was an apologetic tone to his voice.

She snapped her head up to look at him. "You can hear them following us?"

"I heard something back there, yes." He took a minuscule sip of the water bottle before tucking it back into his knapsack. "We can't take any chances, Mia. They could have guns."

He was right, she should have considered that possibility for herself. Truthfully, she'd depended on US Deputy Marshal Sean to keep her safe. She hadn't been forced to take an active role, at least not once she'd gotten to the FBI and then the US Marshals.

Looking back, she should have asked more questions, especially after learning Frankie Junior had taken over his father's illegal business dealings. But she'd assumed the Feds would take care of Frankie.

She sighed and wiped the sweat from her brow. She'd give anything to be back in Cooper's apartment with the opportunity to take a nice cold shower. They had only been gone a few hours, yet it seemed like days had passed since she'd made omelets for breakfast. "How much farther do we need to go?"

"Not sure." He sat down beside her, stretching his legs out in front of him. "Rest for a few minutes, okay?"

She nodded and rested her head back against the tree. Looking up at the sky through the fluttering leaves made her dizzy, so she closed her eyes and tried to relax.

They didn't speak for several long moments. She didn't hear anyone moving through the woods heading toward them, but she knew she could be clueless about that.

Cooper was the expert out here. She was a liability.

"If I remember correctly, there's a trail somewhere in this area," Cooper said softly. "Hopefully, we'll find it."

She turned to look at him. "And if we don't?"

He met her gaze head-on. "We can always head down toward the road. I've stayed away from taking that option in order to avoid stumbling across the black truck."

She frowned. "We've been walking parallel to the road?"

"More or less." Cooper smiled faintly. "I promise I know how to navigate in the woods. I lived in them, remember? We won't get lost."

"I know." She fully trusted him to lead them to safety and wished there was more she could do to help. Other than keeping her mouth shut about how she was tired, hungry, achy, hot, sweaty, and hated every moment of being smothered by flying insects.

"Ready?" He rose gracefully to his feet, offering her his hand.

She clung to his hand, getting clumsily to her feet. The short while they'd stopped to rest had been just enough to make her muscles stiffen up. She forced herself to smile at him. "Okay, let's go."

He surprised her by giving her a quick kiss on the lips before shrugging into his backpack. The kiss had energized her, and had also distracted her, the way he'd likely intended it to.

Cooper led the way, and as the ground sloped beneath her feet, she felt certain they were slowly making their way toward the road. She tried not to get too excited at the thought of being out of the woods.

What was Cooper's plan? Wave down a car? Call another friend to come and pick them up? Hopefully not Suzy who wouldn't be happy to know her car was sitting in some stranger's driveway.

Or did he intend to walk all the way back to Gatlinburg?

Maybe they should try another trip to the police station. Those guys had followed in the truck, they couldn't be watching every single place she and Cooper might go.

Could they?

She'd ditched her phone, but she didn't really know if that was the source of how she'd been found. If so, why not come after them during the night when they'd been at Cooper's apartment? It didn't make any sense.

Yet tossing her phone meant the FBI couldn't return her call. They'd need to call again to leave Cooper's number very soon.

Cooper abruptly stopped in front of her, motioning her to get down. Her muscles tensed as she strained to listen to what had captured his attention.

Then she heard it, the deep rumble of a car engine. No, not a car, maybe a truck.

The black truck with tinted windows? Were the men driving up and down the highway, waiting for them to emerge from the woods?

"You need to stay here," Cooper murmured. "I'm going to check out how far the road is from here."

"Okay." She tried to sound brave and confident when she was anything but.

Cooper slid the knapsack off his shoulders, probably so he could move more freely. She rested her hand on the pack, watching as he moved out of view.

The insects seemed to return with a vengeance, and she wasted precious energy swatting at them.

When a bug flew into her mouth, she gagged and spat it out, trying not to cry.

Get a grip, Mia. You are not going to die from swallowing a bug.

As the minutes ticked by, she strove to remain calm. She very much feared that the longer it took Cooper to return, the less likely he'd bring good news.

If she'd thought hiking through the woods was rough,

she could only imagine how much more difficult it would be to spend the night out here with nothing more than Cooper's knapsack for protection against the elements.

She swallowed hard and prayed. *Please, Lord, keep us safe!*

CHAPTER SEVEN

Cooper inched through the woods, keeping his eye on the ribbon of highway visible through the trees. He wanted to be sure the black truck wasn't lurking around before calling for reinforcements.

The police? He wished he could be certain the cops would bother to come out here to rescue them. Park rangers? That was another possibility.

He was tempted to call a friend, though, rather than going straight to the authorities. He just couldn't shake the fear that these guys might get to Mia before they could reach the sanctuary of the police station.

When he found a good spot with a decent view of the road, he hunkered down to wait. There wasn't a lot of traffic out here, but it didn't take long to hear the sound of an engine, something louder than a car. He wasn't surprised to see a semitruck roll by.

One thing the Preacher had taught them was patience. Cooper didn't move, ignoring the buzz of insects as he waited for the black truck to drive past. He felt certain the two men had given up searching through the woods for them and were most likely parked somewhere along the road, waiting for them to show themselves.

Assuming there had been two men in the truck and not just one.

And how many others? Mia had indicated these guys were part of a big crime ring. Which meant there could be several men out there, watching and waiting.

He and Mia wouldn't get very far on foot. A reluctant smile tugged at the corner of his mouth at how Mia claimed to have flunked out of the Girl Scouts for refusing to use the porta potty.

If they stayed in the woods for much longer, she'd be wishing for the luxury of a porta potty.

His smile faded as he realized how badly he'd failed her. Somehow, these guys had found them in Suzy's car. He had to assume the men had stumbled upon them as they'd headed toward the hotel. Gatlinburg wasn't a large city, but he'd sincerely thought the volume of tourists would help keep them hidden from view.

Unfortunately, his strategy hadn't worked.

And he didn't want to make a similar mistake this time.

Just as he was about to turn around and head back to where he'd left Mia, he heard a car. When a black truck with tinted windows rolled slowly into view, he froze, not even daring to breathe.

There was no way the people inside the truck could see him, but that didn't make the sight of them going past any less menacing. He didn't move until the truck had disappeared from view.

Would they swing back around? Covering this entire stretch of highway knowing he and Mia would want to come out of the woods at some point?

Not good.

He glanced at his phone. There was only one bar, indicating service wasn't great. It was a common problem in the Smoky Mountains. One bar was better than none, but he still wasn't sure who to call.

It was a decision best made with Mia's input. He waited for another ten minutes, waiting for the black truck to swing past again.

His hunch was dead-on. Moments later, the same black truck with tinted windows drove slowly past, coming from the opposite direction. He waited until the truck was out of view before turning to make his way back to Mia.

"Mia?" he called softly as he approached. "Are you okay?"

"I'm so glad you're back." She rose to her feet, swatting at the air. "I was worried something had happened."

"I'm sorry to say the news isn't good." He met her gaze steadily. "The black truck with tinted windows drove by twice. I believe they're waiting for us to come out of the woods."

She paled and sank back down to the ground. "That's terrible."

He hated seeing her like this. He dropped down beside her, taking her hand. "We have a few options, Mia. I have one bar on my phone, so we can call the police, ask them to come pick us up."

Her eyebrows lifted in surprise. "You think they would do that?"

"We can ask." He held her gaze. "We could call another friend of mine, ask her to pick us up. But we'd have to make sure the guys in the truck don't see us."

She grimaced as if she didn't like that plan. "We should try the police first. At some point we'll need to call the FBI office again too."

"Okay. But we need help sooner than later. The last option is for us to keep walking while waiting for darkness to fall. It would be easier to hide from the guys in the truck that way. And they could even give up by then too."

"It's not safe to walk through the woods at night," she protested.

"It's not optimal, no. But it's not that bad. I lived in the woods for weeks, so believe me when I tell you the wildlife is more afraid of us than we are of them."

"Wildlife?" Her voice squeaked. "I was thinking more about tripping and falling."

"Well, there's that risk too. But trust me, we do not want those men to find us. And since they know where we left the car, they know our general location."

She bit her lip and looked away. There was a long moment before she spoke. "Okay, Cooper. Tell me what you think our best option is."

"I say we try the police first. If that doesn't work, we keep walking for a while before calling Chloe for a ride. It's probably best if she picks us up at dusk."

She swallowed hard and nodded. "Okay. I hope Chloe's car is in better shape than Suzy's."

"Me too, although not many of us have cars since we have the trolley and most everything is within reasonable walking distance." He tried not to sound defensive. "So you should know it may not be much better."

"I'm sorry, I didn't mean to imply anything derogatory about your friends." Mia tugged her hand from his. "I know you're doing everything you can to help me, and I really appreciate your efforts."

He sensed her disappointment and couldn't blame her. "When we get back into town, we'll check on the transit station." He hated to admit they should have gone there first. Although he wouldn't put it past these guys to have that location staked out too.

"Okay." Her attempt to smile was rather pathetic. "I, uh, need to go to the bathroom."

"I have some tissues in my backpack." He opened the zipper and rummaged around until he found the crumpled tissues. "Here you go."

"Thanks." She sighed. "This will be a first for me."

"The first of many, right?" His attempt to lighten things up fell flat. "I'll stay here while you find a private spot."

She moved through the woods behind him. He had a couple of PowerBars in his pack but thought they should wait until later to eat them. Unless, of course, they were fortunate enough that the police would actually come to pick them up.

He stared down at his phone for a moment, trying to remember the last time he'd volunteered to contact the police. Yeah, pretty much never. He and Trent had spent a lot of time avoiding the cops, and nearly getting caught was enough to scare him into sketching for money rather than stealing.

But he had to believe the cops would help Mia. After all, she was in serious danger. And the way those guys kept following them was a good indication they were not playing around.

"Remind me to apologize to the Girl Scout leader for my refusing to use the porta potty," Mia said as she walked toward him. "That was far worse. I'm pretty sure a mosquito bit me on my . . ." She sighed. "Never mind. I promised myself no complaining."

"I'm truly sorry about this." He stood and shrugged into his backpack. He used his phone to dial 911, a first for him.

"What's the nature of your emergency?" the dispatcher asked.

"Our car broke down, and we're stranded on the highway," he informed her. "We're also in danger, so if you could send a squad to pick us up, we'd be grateful."

"One moment please."

He glanced at Mia in surprise. "I didn't think 911 operators put people on hold."

"Well, it's not like we're dying," Mia pointed out.

"I guess not." He waited for the operator to return but heard a male voice on the other end of the line.

"This is the Gatlinburg police station, I understand you believe you're in danger?"

Cooper told himself that he was imagining the skepticism in the guy's tone. "Yes, sir. Would you please send a squad to pick us up? We can explain in more detail once we're back at the station."

There was a pause. "Where exactly are you located?"

Cooper gave the guy their estimated location.

"I'm sorry, but we can't give rides to people outside the city limits. We're pretty busy handling issues here. I suggest you call for a tow truck, and if you're in danger, come in to speak to one of the officers on duty."

"There is a black truck with tinted windows driving around looking for us." Cooper couldn't bear to see the disappointment in Mia's eyes. "I'm afraid if we call for a tow truck, they'll find us."

"Do you have a license plate number for the black truck?"

"No." Cooper knew this was a losing battle. "Thanks for your help." Not.

Mia's expression was full of despair. "I take it they're not coming."

He shook his head and slid the phone into his pocket. "Let's keep walking for a while. Being on the move can only help us."

"Lead on," she said wearily.

After seeing the truck driving back and forth on the highway, Cooper felt certain there was no reason for them to worry about being quiet. "You know, I still don't know your real name."

She paused, then said, "My real name is Monique Hastings, but I have to be honest, I've grown accustomed to Mia."

"Mia suits you better than Monique in my opinion."

A smile lifted the corners of her mouth. "Thanks. I wasn't thrilled with Royce, but mainly because I miss my dad and didn't want to give up our last name. I don't think he understood the danger he was in until it was too late."

"I'm sorry for your loss."

She glanced at him in surprise. "How did you know he was dead?"

"An educated guess based on the fact that you're in witness protection." He eyed her thoughtfully. "I'm sure it can't be easy for you to be in a strange city, surrounded by people you don't know."

"It's been difficult," she admitted. "To be honest, I've been pretty much a hermit over these past three months."

"Until you decided to come into town to find a church."

"Yeah." She remained silent for a few minutes. "I guess those men know a little too much about me."

"Who are they?"

She slowly shook her head. "I have no idea what their names are, but I have a suspicion about who sent them." She lifted a hand. "Don't ask me to tell you because you're in enough danger because of me already."

"I don't think knowing the name of the guy trying to find you is going to put me in any more danger than I'm already in," he felt compelled to point out. "You're planning to give the guy's name to the police at some point, right?"

"Yes." She tripped over a log, grabbing onto his back-pack to steady herself. "Although I'd still rather go straight to the FBI."

He tried not to be hurt that she wouldn't confide in him. They walked in silence for a long time before he decided it was time to take another break.

"Let's rest for a while." He gratefully shrugged out of his knapsack. The straps were rubbing painfully against his shoulders, but there was no way in the world he was leaving it behind. "I need to check out the road again, see if the black truck is still patrolling the area." He also needed to use the woods as a bathroom but figured she didn't need to know that part. He pulled out his water bottle. "Here, take a few sips."

She took the water gratefully. "Thanks."

He took a sip too, then recapped the bottle and stuck it in the bag. "I'll be back soon."

"Take your time." For a woman who flunked out of the Girl Scouts, she looked amazingly comfortable sitting against the tree. "I'm glad for the opportunity to rest."

Cooper moved away, heading down the slope toward the road. Soon, he was once again hiding in a thicket, watching for the black truck.

As they'd walked, Cooper had found himself thinking the guys in the black truck would eventually give up and head back into town. How much gas would they waste driving around anyway? Especially knowing they were on foot.

Once he'd assured himself that the truck had given up

and returned to Gatlinburg, he'd call Chloe to come pick them up. Maybe he could convince her to drive them all the way to Knoxville.

On one level, he didn't want to expose Chloe to danger, but if there was any chance of getting out of the city without being followed by the black truck, they needed to take it.

Granted, Chloe would want something from him in return. Like a dinner date. He and Chloe had dated a few times before he'd pulled his usual *let's be friends* card.

Chloe hadn't been happy, but he wanted to believe that wouldn't keep her from helping him out.

Once again, the minutes ticked by slowly. Traffic on the highway was just as sparse as before, but after a solid fifteen minutes of not seeing the black truck, he found himself relaxing.

They must have given up, just as he'd anticipated.

He rose and turned away just as he heard another car approach. He turned in time to see a gray SUV drive past. The fact that the vehicle was moving very slowly, way under the speed limit, made the back of his neck prickle with warning.

Was it possible the occupants were simply admiring the beautiful scenery? No, he wasn't buying it. The way the driver was going so slowly indicated to him that the people inside the SUV were searching for someone.

For them.

Nice trick to change out the vehicle. Cooper eased backward until he felt safe enough to hurry over to where Mia was waiting.

Calling Chloe wasn't an option, at least not yet.

It was beginning to look more and more like they'd be forced to walk all the way out of here. A plan Mia wouldn't like.

Yet it was better than being caught by the men searching for them.

MIA GAVE up swatting at the insects buzzing around her. She'd never imagined she'd be forced to pee in the woods or swallow bugs.

What was next? She honestly didn't want to know.

Her head ached, and she was still incredibly thirsty. Too bad she hadn't jammed food into her small purse. She thought of Cooper's water bottle but held back. He was the expert at surviving in the wilderness, whereas it was taking all her willpower not to run away screaming at the top of her lungs.

Scratch that. She was too tired, too hungry, and too thirsty to run anywhere. Or to scream.

This situation was mostly her fault. If she'd followed Sean's instructions to avoid things she'd routinely done in her previous life, Frankie's men wouldn't have found her.

Yet, the fact that she'd heard absolutely nothing from her marshal contact was ominous enough that her location had likely been compromised anyway. And if she followed that reasoning, going to church had saved her life because Cooper had noticed her and had protected her.

She'd been taught that God always had a plan. It was time for her to stop second-guessing His will. She was alive and unharmed, if you didn't count the blisters on her feet, and that was a blessing she needed to be grateful for.

Mia closed her eyes and tried to relax. Obviously, Cooper was taking frequent rest breaks for her sake. She felt certain that once he verified the black truck was no longer in the area, he'd call his friend Chloe, another woman of course, to pick them up.

Didn't Cooper have any male friends? She could easily understand why females flocked to him, he was talented and drop-dead gorgeous, but surely there were guys in the area too.

She must have dozed a bit because Cooper's voice roused her.

"Mia? Are you okay?" He dropped to his knees beside her, running his hands over her arms and up to her face.

"Yes, why?" She knew she looked disheveled after hiking in the woods for the past hour or so, but she was now suddenly self-conscious. "Don't I look okay?"

"I thought you passed out." Cooper sank back onto his heels. "I—you just scared me, that's all."

His concern was touching. "Well, I'm fine." It was surprisingly true. "Did you see the black truck again?"

"No, but a dark gray SUV drove by extremely slowly." His expression was grim. "I sat and waited, sure enough, it drove back the other way just as slowly." He shook his head. "I'm sorry, Mia, but I have a feeling they swapped vehicles as a way to throw us off."

She sighed. "I have to give Frankie more credit, I didn't realize he'd be so smart."

"Frankie?" he echoed, arching his brow.

"Frankie Germaine Junior," she admitted. Keeping her secret seemed ridiculous at this point. Cooper was right, he was already in danger, and knowing who'd hired the men wouldn't lessen the danger.

Frankie would assume she'd told Cooper everything regardless. Making her feeble attempt to protect him seem ridiculous.

"Frankie Junior makes me think of a little kid." Cooper

flashed a cheeky grin. "You'd think he'd go by his middle name or something."

"Yeah, but I'm sure his being in a mobster family kept the teasing at bay." She rose to her feet. "I only have Sean's word that Frankie took over his father's business, but it makes sense he'd be the one to come after me." She glanced around. "So now what?"

"We keep walking." Cooper grimaced. "I wish I had a better option."

She couldn't deny the thought of more walking made her want to groan, but she forced herself to nod. "It's okay. We're alive, and that's what matters."

He grimaced as he slid his arms through the straps of his knapsack. "That's a nice positive attitude you have there, Mia."

"I'm trying," she admitted. "Do you want me to carry the pack for a while?"

"No, it's my pack, my responsibility." He hesitated, then added, "I really don't want to leave it behind."

"I'd never ask you to do that." She gestured for him to head out. "I'm following you, remember? If I was in charge, we'd get lost for sure."

"You need to give yourself more credit," Cooper pointed out. "Remember, I told you we're heading parallel to the road. It's not that difficult if you listen for the traffic, making sure it's to your right the entire time. Plus, keep an eye on the sun, that will also help you know which direction to take."

"I guess I could probably do that," she admitted. "Can I borrow your phone to call the FBI?"

"Sure, but let's wait until we're out of the woods, the reception might be better."

They continued walking for what seemed like days instead

of hours. Every so often Cooper would stop and offer sips of water. She was impressed that he'd lived in the woods for weeks, considering she was having trouble lasting a few hours. When she thought she wouldn't be able to take another step, Cooper stopped to rest and brought a PowerBar out of his backpack.

"We'll split this, okay?" He unwrapped the bar, bent it in half, and gave her the larger portion.

She was embarrassed at how quickly she wolfed it down, not to mention the length of time she spent licking her fingers. When she finally finished, she glanced sheepishly at him. "Thanks."

"You're welcome." He handed her the water bottle that was now only a quarter full. "We're going to need to find a stream soon."

She was so thirsty that even a mountain stream teeming with bugs sounded good. "Maybe we should check to see if the gray SUV is still out there?"

Cooper didn't say anything for a moment as he replaced the water bottle in his pack. "I'm not sure we should bank on the fact that they're still using the gray SUV. For all we know, they could have swapped that out for something different."

Logically she knew he was right, but that didn't mean she liked it. "Then what? Are we walking all the way back to Gatlinburg? And if that is your plan, won't we have to walk on the road at some point?"

"We walk until dark, and then I'll call for Chloe to pick us up. She generally works the early shifts anyway, so she'll be off by then. Hopefully, we'll be far enough away from where we abandoned Suzy's car that Germaine's men won't notice."

She sighed. His so-called plan was slightly better than

walking all the way back to Gatlinburg. Her feet were already screaming in pain, but she managed to ignore them. "Okay, let's go."

Cooper caught her up in a surprising hug. She wrapped her arms around his waist and hugged him back.

"You've been so wonderful through this, Mia," he whispered in her ear.

"Not me, you," she corrected. "I'd never have made it this far on my own."

He grinned and gave her a kiss that was over before she had the chance to truly appreciate it. "We make a great team."

The euphoria from his embrace didn't last long. All too soon she was wincing with every step and swallowing hard against her scratchy, dry throat.

Finally, Cooper lifted his hand, indicating they could take another break. "The sun is starting to go down," he said as he shared his water bottle. "I think we should be able to call Chloe in a couple of hours."

Hours? She tried not to cry.

At their next break, Cooper found a stream. Mia followed his lead, sticking her hands and her face into the water. She didn't care if there were zillions of bugs in there, the cool water felt wonderful against her hot, dry, sticky skin.

If Cooper hadn't been there, she'd have stripped down to her birthday suit and gone all the way in.

"I have one more PowerBar we can share," he announced when they were finished drinking from the stream.

"Sneaky that you didn't mention you had two of them earlier," she teased. The water had refreshed her attitude as well. If her feet didn't hurt so badly, she'd have enjoyed this time with Cooper.

He flashed a grin and broke the PowerBar in half. "We'll walk another ninety minutes, then make the call to Chloe. We'll need to find a meeting spot recognizable from the road."

After the long day, ninety minutes actually sounded doable. "Maybe we can find a street sign or something."

"I'm sure we will," he agreed.

They ate in silence. When it was time to leave, Mia shifted her purse to her back and stretched out to drink from the stream, bathing her face and hands before slowly rising to her feet. "That was nice, Cooper. Thanks."

He lifted a brow. "I didn't create the stream."

"No, God did that. But you found it for us. Maybe with God's help."

He frowned but remained silent. His lack of faith was troubling, but she didn't push.

They walked on as the sun continued to edge down on the horizon. The trees overhead blocked much of the sunlight, which was a blessing. They headed down the slope, presumably in the general direction of the road. Finally, Cooper came to a stop. Peering between the trees, she was surprised to see a small stretch of a blacktop road.

"We need a landmark before I call Chloe." He glanced at her. "I need you to check out the road heading in the direction from where we came while I look up ahead."

She swallowed hard. "Okay."

They drifted apart, moving slowly through the woods. The closer she got to the road, the tighter her nerves stretched. What if Frankie's men were still driving back and forth looking for them? What if they grabbed her before Cooper even knew she was gone?

Twin headlights coming around a curve had her ducking down behind a tree. Her heart pounded, but once the vehicle passed, she relaxed. It hadn't been a truck or an SUV but a dark sedan. The car had gone by fast, so she highly doubted it was anyone searching for them.

She found a highway marker, memorized the numbers, and quickly headed back to their meeting spot. Upon seeing Cooper, she was proud of herself for not getting lost. "Highway marker 762."

He grinned. "That's way better than the yield sign I found. Good job." He pulled out his phone. "Hey, Chloe, it's Cooper. I need a big favor."

Mia listened as Cooper explained where they were. When he lowered his phone, he gave a nod. "She's on her way. Let's get down to that marker you found."

Retracing her steps wasn't nearly as easy, and she overshot the highway marker. When they found it, Cooper led her to a hiding spot a few feet away.

For long moments, neither of them spoke. "How far away is she?" Mia finally asked.

"Only ten minutes or so, we covered more ground than I expected." He glanced at her. "She has a white Chevy Malibu."

"Got it."

Fifteen minutes later, another pair of headlights came into view. This car was going much slower, and for a minute, she feared the worst. Then it pulled off to the side of the road.

It was a white sedan. Cooper rose and offered his hand. They scrambled from their hiding spot and approached the car.

"Coop?" A female voice drifted toward them. Then the

tone sharpened. "Who's with you? I thought you were alone?"

Mia tensed and glanced at Cooper who looked guilty at being caught in an untruth. Chloe crossed her arms over her chest and scowled.

Mia's spirits sank.

They were so close to being taken to safety, only now she had a bad feeling it wouldn't take much for Chloe to abruptly drive off, leaving them behind.

CHAPTER EIGHT

Cooper inwardly groaned at Chloe's peevish attitude. He was tired, hungry, achy, and so not in the mood for this.

"Geez, Cooper, don't you have any guy friends?" Mia asked in a low voice.

He shrugged, forced a smile, and summoned the strength to smooth things over. He approached the woman he considered a friend, hoping she wouldn't change her mind about helping them out. "Hi, Chloe, thanks for coming. This is Mia, I was giving her a lift to Knoxville when the car I borrowed died. We've been hiking through the woods for hours now, so I'm really glad you agreed to come pick us up."

Chloe's scowl only deepened. "I still don't understand why you didn't mention you were here with someone."

He knew she really meant that he hadn't mentioned being with a woman. Because if he'd been out here with Trent, or any other guy, Chloe wouldn't have been threatened the way she was now. Frankly, this was exactly why he hadn't mentioned Mia to Chloe in the first place. And why did Chloe care if he was here with Mia anyway? It wasn't as if they'd dated recently.

He decided to try another tactic. "Chloe, I didn't think it mattered. I know you're not the kind of person who would leave two people stranded in the woods all night."

Her eyes narrowed, and he could tell his subtle barb hit home. "I'm not." Her tone was still defensive, but she stepped forward to open the back passenger door. "You just caught me by surprise, that's all. I'm here, so you and Mia may as well get in."

"Thank you." Mia spoke softly as she stepped forward to slide into the rear passenger seat. She quickly closed the door, forcing Cooper to sit up front next to Chloe.

"I owe you for this, thanks." He slid into the passenger seat. "I, uh, Mia still needs to get to Knoxville. Any chance you'd be willing to drive us there?"

Chloe shot him a glance. "I have to work early tomorrow morning, so no."

Ouch. Okay, then. He knew it had been a long shot anyway. Chloe was clearly not happy, but she needed to understand this wasn't a joyride. "Listen, I know it's asking a lot, but this is important—"

"No, it's not a big deal, Cooper," Mia cut in. "I can wait until tomorrow. We talked about me getting there another way, remember?"

He glanced over his shoulder. Mia was giving him a look that warned him not to go into detail about the danger they were facing. And he understood she didn't want to drag Chloe into harm's way, but getting out of Gatlinburg and to the FBI office in Knoxville was more important than worrying about whether or not Junior's men would find out.

"It is important," he insisted.

"No, my being stranded in Gatlinburg isn't Chloe's

problem." There was a note of steel underlining her tone. "She was kind enough to pick us up tonight, that's more than we can ask for. I'll find a way to get to Knoxville."

"If I didn't work the early shift, I'd consider taking you tonight." Chloe sounded more like herself now, so maybe she was getting over her annoyance. "But the drive would take at least an hour each way, and unfortunately, I have to be up at four thirty in order to get to work by five."

"I know you generally work the early shifts." Her schedule, along with being one of the few people he knew who owned a car, had been the reason he'd reached out to her. Cooper decided to let it go. Maybe Mia was right about not explaining about the danger. He felt bad enough deceiving Chloe about picking him up as it was.

"You can take a taxi to Knoxville," Chloe added. "It's expensive, but you wouldn't have to worry about a car conking out on you."

"We'll look into that option," Cooper said.

"Again, thank you for doing this, Chloe," Mia added. "You really are a lifesaver." Mia's sincerity seemed to thaw what was left of Chloe's animosity.

Chloe nodded. "Where do you want me to drop you off?"

"At the mass transit center," Mia quickly interjected before he had a chance to respond. "I assume that's where the taxi drivers hang out, right?"

"Yes, but probably not this late. The taxi service is centered around going from the airport in Knoxville to here and back." Chloe glanced at him. "Do you want me to take you to your place?"

"Uh, no thanks, I can walk from the transit station." He smiled. "You need to go home and get some sleep."

"Yeah." Chloe looked skeptical, as if there was a deeper

reason he wanted to stay with Mia, but she didn't pursue the issue. Instead, she slowed down as they approached the downtown area of Gatlinburg. "But your apartment isn't that much farther."

"I know." Cooper waved his hand. "Really, you can drop us off anywhere nearby. Whatever is easier for you."

"Okay." Chloe took him at his word and pulled over after a couple of blocks. "Will I see you tomorrow, Coop?"

"I'll stop in for coffee after getting Mia to Knoxville," he agreed. "Thanks again, Chloe. I really owe you one."

"Yes, thank you, Chloe." Mia quickly slid out of the back seat.

Seconds later, Chloe had pulled away from the curb, leaving them standing in the road. Cooper felt vulnerable out in the open and glanced around to make sure none of Junior's men were nearby.

"You didn't really want to go to the transit center, did you?" he asked Mia in a low tone.

"Yeah, I really did." Mia shoved her hair out of her face. "Although I didn't realize the taxi service might not be readily available. So now what?"

"I think we should wait until morning." He tugged her arm, drawing her away from the side of the road to the shadows of a building. "We'll call the FBI office again, but I'm not holding my breath they'll respond very quickly. I think I can convince Chloe to drive us to Knoxville after she gets off work tomorrow."

"Yeah, I'm sure she'll be happy enough to see the last of me," Mia said dryly.

He was glad the darkness hid his blush. "I never promised Chloe anything," he protested.

"I'm sure you didn't, which is likely the problem." Mia

sighed. "Why do they call it a mass transit center when there is no mass transit?"

"I don't know. The trolley goes all around town, and all the way to Pigeon Forge, but there's no bus station there either." He stood in the shadows, understanding Mia's desire to put all of this behind her. They'd been running from Junior's thugs for the past two days, and it was wearing her down.

Him too, but he was still determined to keep Mia safe.

No matter what.

"I guess I really am stranded here," Mia said on a sigh. "I didn't realize this place was cut off from the other cities."

"It's not cut off, exactly, but I can see what you mean. Driving is the only way out of here. Let's head back to my place," Cooper urged. Maybe his paranoia was getting the better of him, but he didn't like being out in the open. And he needed to call Suzy about her car and a tow truck to have it picked up. "We need to get showered, eat, and get some rest."

"Sounds good." Mia looked dead on her feet.

He admired her strength and determination. He led her around the corner of the building and down a deserted street in a roundabout way to get back to his apartment. These were areas the tourists didn't routinely hang out, and at nine o'clock at night, they'd be sticking to Main Street and the well-known pubs.

Skirting around the next building, he paused and looked up ahead. So far, so good.

He led the way down another street, then cut through an alley. Soon they were only two blocks away from his apartment.

Swallowing hard, he cut between two buildings until they were behind the apartment. There was no sign of

Junior's men or the black truck with tinted windows or the gray SUV.

Still, he couldn't ignore the itch along the back of his neck. Junior's men had picked up their tail while he'd been driving Suzy's car.

Was it possible they'd also discovered where he lived?

"Cooper?" Mia's tone was hushed.

He glanced at her, then eased the pack from his aching shoulders. "Keep your eyes open," he warned as he dug for his keys.

Key in hand, he glanced around one last time before lifting his knapsack and moving toward the back door. Seconds later, they were inside the building.

The hallways were relatively well lit, if you didn't count the scattering of broken lightbulbs. The light hurt his eyes after being in the dark for what seemed like an eternity. He moved quickly to his door, unlocked it, and stepped inside. Mia followed, and he quickly closed and locked the door behind them.

The place looked exactly as they'd left it. Still, he set the pack on the floor and moved carefully through the small space to make sure no one was lying in wait.

"It's clear," he said, returning to the kitchen. "Shut off the light, would you?" He lit a candle on the table, then glanced around. "We need to eat, although I'm afraid all I can offer is another frozen pizza."

"I'm okay with that," Mia said. "I'm famished, but I would rather shower first, if you don't mind."

"Go ahead. The pizza should be ready by the time you're finished." He pulled it from the freezer. "Wait, I'll grab a fresh T-shirt for you to wear."

"That would be wonderful," she said gratefully.

He set the pizza down and hurried into his room. He

found a clean shirt and gave it to her. "Sorry I don't have anything more."

"This is fine, thanks." Mia moved toward the bathroom, then stopped. "I'm sorry about Suzy's car. I'm sure she's not going to be happy to hear we left it behind. Once I get access to my bank accounts, I can help pay for the towing fee."

"Don't worry about it." Cooper offered a wry smile. "Our priority right now is to get you safely to the FBI."

She nodded and slipped into the bathroom. Cooper expelled a heavy breath and tossed the pizza into the oven. He guzzled a bottle of water, then sank into a chair, trying not to moan out loud.

He hadn't hiked for an entire day in years and was obviously badly out of shape. Sketching wasn't exactly physically demanding unless you counted the slight strain on his hands and arms. He'd gotten soft over the years, that was for sure. He quickly called Suzy, glad when he was sent to voice mail. He realized he couldn't call the towing company without a firm location of the car. That task would have to wait.

Cooper closed his eyes and tried to relax.

Don't you have any guy friends?

Mia's question rankled. As much as he hated to admit it, he didn't have many close friends, period. And those he had were all female. Why? He couldn't say. Maybe because he liked art and didn't really care much about sports or cars.

Or maybe he hadn't been able to connect with another guy after Trent had taken off for Nashville.

Without giving himself time to think about it, he stood and pulled his phone from his pocket. The battery was running low, so he plugged it in and made the call. He found himself holding his breath as he listened to the ringing on the other end of the line.

Trent didn't pick up, but Cooper was instructed by a mechanical voice to leave a message. He spoke quickly. "Trent? It's Coop. I could use some help if you have time. It's kinda a long story, so call me back at this number, okay? Thanks." He rattled off the number, then set his phone aside.

Would his foster brother return his call? Cooper wasn't at all convinced.

For one thing, Trent played lead guitar for the Jimmy Woodrow Band, and they were pretty good. By now, they could be playing in some swanky joint in Nashville for a crowd of enthusiastic fans.

He didn't begrudge his foster brother the success he deserved. Trent lived for his music the way he needed his art. Gatlinburg wasn't the music metropolis Nashville was.

Should he have gone with Trent? It was a choice he'd often thought about. How different his life might be if he had?

Then again, if he'd left Gatlinburg, what would have happened to Mia? Junior's men would have grabbed her and taken her away and likely killed her.

The thought strengthened his determination to push forward. No one had really needed him, not the way Mia did.

He wasn't going to waste another second thinking about the decisions he'd made in the past.

Even though he secretly cherished every moment he was able to spend with her, it was better to stay focused on getting Mia safely out of Gatlinburg.

Before Junior's men found them once more.

MIA FORCED herself not to linger in the shower, although the cool water felt incredible against her weary muscles. Cooper needed to clean up too.

She wrinkled her nose at wearing the same under-clothes, but Cooper's shirt smelled wonderful. She held the fabric to her face, inhaling his musky scent.

Okay, enough. Get a grip, she wasn't some goofy woman in the middle of a fabric softener commercial. Just because Cooper had saved her life, more than once, didn't mean she should allow her emotions to run amok.

The guy only had girlfriends, which was an indication he preferred to play the field. And after seeing how Rachel, Suzy, and now Chloe had acted upon seeing her, it was clear that Cooper didn't do serious relationships.

A fact that she'd do well to remember.

After she was dressed, she ran a comb through her wet hair and left the bathroom. The enticing scent of pizza greeted her, and her stomach rumbled in response. Cooper glanced over at her and grinned.

"Hey, the pizza should be ready soon."

"Do you want to take a shower before you eat?" She removed a glass from the cupboard and poured herself a large glass of water. Despite the water she'd already ingested, she knew that her body still needed to be rehydrated.

He raked his fingers through his hair and grimaced. "I'll wait till we're finished eating."

She downed half the water, then pulled out two plates. Eerie that she felt at home here, despite only knowing Cooper for two days.

It seemed like a lifetime.

"It's ready," he announced. He donned oven mitts and pulled it out. From there, he sliced it and set it in the center of the table, near the candle.

"I'd like to pray, if that's okay." Mia glanced at him curiously.

"Okay." He surprised her by clasping his hands together and bowing his head.

"Dear Lord, thank You for protecting us from harm and leading us to safety. We are humbly grateful at how You continue to watch over us. Please continue to lead us on Your chosen path. Amen."

"Amen."

Cooper's whispered *Amen* brought a rush of happiness. She lifted her head, smiled at him, and teased, "Time to dig in."

He grinned and gestured to the pizza. "Ladies first."

She helped herself to a slice and took a bite. "Yeah, I'm sure Chloe is still smarting over how you tricked her into picking us up." She shook her head. "What were you thinking?"

He shrugged as he took some pizza. "I didn't trick her, I just didn't tell her everything."

She snorted. "Same difference."

He didn't say anything for a long moment, each busy wolfing down their meal. "You were right, I don't have a lot of guy friends," he admitted. "But I called my foster brother, Trent, and left a message asking if he might be able to help us out."

She lifted a brow. "And Trent is where exactly?"

"Nashville."

"That means he's more than four hours away." She tossed her fork aside and picked up her pizza with her fingers. Nothing had ever tasted so good.

"I know, but it's nice to have a backup plan." Cooper took another bite. "I'm sorry my initial plan was a dud."

It wasn't his fault Suzy's car died. Or that the FBI hadn't returned her call before she was forced to ditch the phone. She'd borrow Cooper's phone to call again, but honestly, she was too exhausted to care. Her entire body ached as if she'd run a marathon instead of a long walk through the woods.

Mia cleaned up the kitchen as Cooper took his turn in the shower. She used his phone and made a second call to the FBI, leaving his number instead of her old one. Then she blew out the candle and sat in the dark on the living room sofa.

Cooper had opened up to her about his life with the Preacher but hadn't said much else about his foster family. She found herself wishing she could spend more time with him, uncovering what really made him tick.

Other than his art, which was incredible.

But man could not live on art alone, and it occurred to her that Cooper might be using his art as a way to keep the rest of the world at bay. To see people only as interesting faces he needed to sketch rather than allowing any of them to get too close.

A defense mechanism from the time he'd spent living with the Preacher? Probably. She was secretly glad the Preacher couldn't hurt Cooper or any of the other kids anymore. The man who'd spewed blasphemy about God as he abused young children didn't deserve to survive the fire.

As soon as the thought went through her mind, she winced. God taught them to forgive those who trespassed against them. And she knew that was the right thing to do. But forgiving the Preacher for what he put Cooper and the other kids through wouldn't be easy.

Especially not for those kids who'd suffered at his hands.

She sent up a prayer asking God to watch over all the foster kids who'd been harmed by the man. At times like this, she could understand why Cooper had a hard time believing.

Which only made his response to her prayer at dinner all the more amazing.

A sense of peace washed over her, and she relaxed further into the sofa cushions.

"Mia?"

She started and opened her eyes. From the bit of light coming through the curtains, she could see Cooper was standing beside her. "What?"

He smiled. "Sorry, I didn't mean to wake you. Why don't you head to bed? It's been a long day."

"I can sleep on the sofa. You deserve to sleep in your own bed."

"Nah, I like the sofa." He held out his hand. "Come on, I'll help you up."

"I'm not a hundred years old," she groused, taking his hand. The way her muscles protested made her realize her body felt like she was more than a century old.

"My muscles are sore too," he confided as he gently pulled her up to her feet. "I can offer you some ibuprofen."

"I'm fine." At least, she figured she'd feel better after getting some rest. Cooper's fingers curled warmly around hers, and she reveled in the sensation. Despite knowing he'd likely bruised the hearts of the women he'd insisted were just friends, she found herself drawn to him in a way she'd never experienced before.

She would miss him.

"Good night, Mia," he murmured as they reached the door to his room.

"Good night, Cooper." She forced herself to release him and move away before she could give in to the temptation to kiss him.

Thankfully, he was a gentleman and turned away, leaving her to close the door between them. She blew out a breath and climbed into bed.

Last night, which seemed like weeks ago, Cooper had woken her up by calling out in the middle of a nightmare. She sent up a silent prayer that he'd be able to sleep tonight without having bad dreams.

Sheer exhaustion lulled her into a deep sleep. But a strange noise roused her, making her frown into the darkness.

Pushing herself upright, she strained to listen. Were the sounds coming from the apartment next door? Funny, she couldn't remember hearing any of Cooper's neighbors before now.

Maybe she just hadn't been paying attention.

Now that she was awake, she needed to use the bathroom. She slid out of bed and pulled the edge of Cooper's shirt down over her bottom. She eased the door open, then changed her mind and quickly pulled on her jeans. Call her crazy, but she couldn't walk around his apartment barely dressed. Feeling better, she eased the door open and glanced around. The rest of the apartment was dark as Cooper was likely still sleeping.

Unless the noises she heard were from him having another nightmare?

She tiptoed out to the main living space. When she found Cooper sprawled on the sofa, sound asleep, she relaxed and turned back to the bathroom.

When she was finished in the bathroom, she heard the noise again. What in the world was it? Not people talking, but more like a weird thumping noise. Or maybe a dragging noise.

Or maybe just her overactive imagination.

Mia hesitated in the hallway, debating with herself. Should she wake Cooper to find out if he knew the origin of the weird noise? The poor guy deserved to get an uninterrupted night's sleep.

The noise came again, louder this time. She froze. Was it coming from the hallway outside the apartment door?

She crept back into the living room and found Cooper had woken up. "Stay back," he whispered.

Okay, now she was really alarmed. She eased backward, secretly grateful she'd pulled on her jeans. She watched as Cooper silently approached the apartment door to look through the peephole.

When he reared back, her pulse spiked. "Someone's out there. We have to go."

"Go where?" She asked the question even though she knew there wasn't really a good answer. He grabbed his knapsack, pulled his phone from the charger, and stuffed his feet into running shoes.

"Hurry," he urged, steering her into his bedroom.

She took a moment to pull on her shoes. She grabbed her purse and took only the cash before joining him at the window. Thankfully, they were on the first floor, but she sensed it wouldn't matter if they weren't. Clearly Cooper's plan was to go out the window regardless.

He slid the window up and turned toward her. "We need to hurry."

She quickly threw one leg over the sill, ducked beneath, and then eased the rest of the way out. Once she was on solid ground, she pressed herself against the building, glancing around frantically.

She'd ditched her phone if that's how she'd been tracked before.

So how had Frankie's men found them again?

CHAPTER NINE

Cooper moved swiftly and silently along the side of the building, keeping Mia tucked behind him. His choices were limited, so he could only hope he'd picked the right direction, far away from where Junior's men might be waiting and watching. He inwardly railed at himself for not finding a different place for them to stay. Logically, it made sense that Junior's goons would eventually find out where he lived.

A dark shadow moved up ahead. He froze, feeling the slight pressure as Mia bumped into him from behind.

The shadow shifted again, revealing the barest hint of a dark shape similar to that of a tall man. A guy he felt certain was one of Junior's thugs.

What were the odds they'd stumble across another bad guy looking to rob people?

Cooper shifted slightly, easing the pack from his shoulders. As if reading his mind, Mia took the weight of the knapsack, silently lowering it to the ground. He didn't have much in the way of a weapon, but he managed to slide one of his slender colored pencils from his pack.

It wasn't much, but it was better than nothing.

He pressed a hand against Mia's arm, a gesture that indicated she should stay put. She briefly covered his hand with hers as if she understood. Barely daring to breathe, Cooper took a step forward, then another.

Other than the colored pencil, the only other advantage he had was the element of surprise. If he could catch the guy off guard long enough to disable him.

Before he was shot.

He didn't think much about his imminent demise. His main concern was to distract the guy long enough for Mia to get away. Even if that meant sacrificing himself in order to make that happen.

The shadow moved again; he was standing at the corner of the building now. It seemed as if the guy was growing impatient with the delay. Cooper could relate, he knew the guy in the hallway would be inside his apartment any minute. There wasn't a moment to waste, yet he also needed to get close enough to strike.

When the guy turned toward him, Cooper knew the gig was up. He lunged forward, stabbing at the man's face with the pencil even as he braced for the impact of a bullet or a knife.

By some miracle he managed to catch the guy off guard. The man stumbled backward, yelling out in pain as the sharpened end of the pencil struck its mark near his eye. Cooper didn't let up, kicking and punching the guy until he was on the ground.

Cooper was about to head back toward Mia when she appeared at his side, swinging the knapsack to hit the man on the head. He was shocked she'd done that, but there wasn't a second to waste. He grabbed her hand and began to run. This time, silence wasn't critical. They desperately needed to get far away from the scene of the crime.

He took her through one parking lot, then another. The trolley only ran until midnight, so there was no chance to use it as an escape route at three in the morning.

There weren't many people out and about at this time of the night either.

When he heard Mia breathing hard, he slowed and found a place to hide out and rest for a few minutes. He belatedly realized she'd been lugging his knapsack the entire time.

"You brought it with you?" he asked in a surprise whisper. "I'd have thought you'd have tossed it aside."

"It—has—your—art—supplies," she gasped between words.

"They're not more important than your life, Mia." It was the first time he'd uttered such a bold statement, but it was true. His art supplies could easily be replaced.

Mia couldn't.

He slid his arms into the straps of the knapsack, ignoring the way his muscles protested, and glanced around. "We'll need to find a place to stay for what's left of the night." A strategy he should have considered before now.

"Will any of these motels take cash?" Mia asked in a whisper.

He hesitated, then shrugged. "Only one way to find out."

Her expression was grim, but really, what choice did they have? Other than possibly trying to head back to the police station. But he didn't want to do that now in case they stumbled across Junior's men.

Besides, the police station was likely locked up tight at this hour of the night.

Cooper tried to remember where he and Trent had ended up all those years ago. Was the cheap motel still there? He wasn't sure as he hadn't made it a habit to keep up on the local news.

All that he'd cared about was catering to the tourists to make money. A pretty sad existence now that he thought about it.

There would be time to ruminate on his mistakes later. He estimated they were roughly a mile from the motel. Not a far distance, except that they'd put on several miles already and hadn't gotten much sleep.

"This way," he murmured, heading off down another street. To her credit, Mia kept up without a problem. Apparently being out of breath was mostly because she'd been lugging his knapsack.

A humbling gesture of support he wasn't sure he deserved.

Cooper kept to the shadows while moving as fast as he dared. They were living on borrowed time. Junior's men would likely be driving around, in who knew what kind of car, searching for them.

A police squad pulled up in front of a tavern where a group of people were milling about. Possibly the result of a bar fight. Cooper used the distraction to pick up their pace.

"Maybe we should go back and talk to those officers," Mia whispered.

He slowed and glanced at her. "You think so?"

"I don't know," she confessed. "I mean, I'm sure they're busy with whatever they were called about, but there's still a chance they'd offer to take us in."

Cooper had spent a night or two in jail and wasn't eager

to repeat the experience. He hesitated, knowing she was right to consider going to the cops. It was something he'd thought of trying again too. And approaching a squad that is out on patrol would be better than trying to get all the way back to the station.

"Let's keep our eyes open for another police car," he said. "Maybe one that isn't in the middle of breaking up a bar fight."

"Okay," she agreed.

As they continued making their way to the motel, he hoped he wasn't steering Mia down the wrong path. Was he really following his gut instincts? Or was he keeping her with him for selfish reasons?

He was afraid it was the latter.

The sign for the motel came into view. Thankfully, he could see the vacancy light was on, which was a relief considering it was still tourist season.

Then again, tourists didn't really flock to Gatlinburg to stay at a two-star establishment such as this one.

He paused in the shadows catty-corner from the motel to pull out his cash. He'd pulled some money out of his coffee can before going out to borrow Suzy's car. But getting a room now meant they'd end up paying for two nights, and he knew bribe money may be needed to get the clerk to accept cash.

"I brought what was left of my cash," Mia said as he went through the bills he'd pulled from his pocket.

"Keep it for now, we may need that to get a taxi to Knoxville." He put some of the bills back into his pocket. "Are you ready to give this a shot?"

A half smile tugged at the corner of her mouth. "Yep. Let's do it."

After sweeping his gaze over the area one more time,

he took her hand and broke into a light jog. When he realized he was holding his breath, he called himself an idiot and breathed in a gulp of air as they reached the lobby door.

The place was locked, but there was a buzzer on the outside. He hit the buzzer, then pressed his face against the glass door to look inside.

An older man in his late sixties or early seventies moved his hand beneath the counter. A second later, there was a loud click as the door unlocked. Cooper gratefully pulled it open and gestured for Mia to go inside.

"Kinda late to be lookin' fer a room," the man said, obviously annoyed at being interrupted from whatever he was doing to stay awake.

"I'm so sorry," Mia said, stepping forward and smiling at him. "We went for a hike and got lost in the woods. Our cell phone didn't work, so we had to walk all the way back." She gazed up at him, her face full of sweet innocence. "Would you be so kind as to give us a room? My feet are killing me. I have blisters on my blisters."

Cooper had to give her credit. Her story sounded legit, and the old man's skeptical expression softened. "You hiked all that way in the dark? It's lucky you didn't break a leg."

"I ate a bug." Mia shuddered. "It was nasty. I'm really looking forward to running water and a bathroom. Will you please give us a room?"

Her comment made the old man chuckle. If Cooper hadn't seen the guy's transformation for himself, he might not have believed it. "Yeah, sure. I can give you a room, but checkout time is ten thirty, so you won't be able to stay long."

"Oh, thank you." Mia reached across the desk to lightly touch the man's arm. "You're so sweet to help us out."

"That yer boyfriend?" The old man eyed him specu-latively.

"Yes, although I have to admit, I may need to rethink this relationship since Charles doesn't seem to have a very good sense of direction." Mia smiled teasingly, and Cooper lifted a brow at the name she'd bestowed on him.

Charles? What did he look like, the Prince of England?

He shook it off and stepped forward setting several twenty-dollar bills on the counter. "We don't have any credit cards, will you consider taking cash?"

Now the old man looked suspicious. "You have ID?"

Cooper held his gaze. "Afraid not, we didn't bring them along on our hike."

There was a long stretch of silence as the old man considered his proposition. "Charles? Or do you go by Chuck?"

"Charles," he said without hesitation. He set another twenty-dollar bill down. "Please, sir, Mary is exhausted. We can't walk another step." He leaned forward. "And she really, really needs to use the bathroom."

The old man scooped up the money and handed them two keys. "Room 107, but don't forget checkout time is ten thirty."

"We won't forget," Mia said, flashing a grateful smile. "Thanks again."

Cooper nodded at the guy as he handed Mia one of the keys. Pretending to be a couple was the smart thing to do, asking for two rooms would have raised questions, not to mention would have cost twice as much.

They left the lobby and hurried down the brightly lit sidewalk to their room. It wasn't until they were safely inside the room with the door shut and the dead bolt clicked into place that Cooper dared to relax. He ran his hands through his hair and dropped the knapsack to the floor.

"Nice job, Mia." The room didn't smell great, but the fact that there were two beds made up for the musty scent.

"I didn't like lying to him," she said honestly. "I used enough of the real truth to embellish our story, which helped." She grimaced. "I hope God won't hold the lie against me."

The Preacher's God would, but he didn't voice that thought. Mia claimed the Preacher's view of God wasn't accurate, so he left it alone. "No way would that guy have given me a room without you sweet-talking him."

She sank down onto the edge of the bed. "It's hard to believe we managed to escape Frankie's men for the third time in twenty-four hours."

"Yeah." This recent turn of events proved their options were limited. Either take a taxi all the way to Knoxville to the FBI office or find a way to get to the local police.

Either way, they couldn't afford to linger in the area much longer. They had in fact already stayed longer than they should have.

A hard lump of guilt lodged in the back of his throat. He'd nearly failed Mia, not once but several times.

If Junior's men had gotten to her, he'd only have had himself to blame.

THE ENORMITY of what had happened at Cooper's apartment hit hard. Mia had to twist her fingers together to keep them from trembling. This was the second time in a matter of days that Cooper had been forced to attack Frankie's men.

All because of her.

Mia abruptly jumped to her feet and dashed into the bathroom. She closed and locked the door, then sank onto the commode, burying her face in her hands.

Dear Lord, what have I done?

They couldn't keep going like this. She knew it and so did Cooper. The guilt in his eyes had only made her feel worse. This was her problem, not his. She should have figured out a way to get out of Gatlinburg earlier, without dragging Cooper along and placing him in danger. He'd saved her life, more than once, but watching him attack that man with nothing more than a pencil had scared her. If Frankie's hired gun had hurt him, or worse, she wouldn't have been able to forgive herself.

Drawing in a deep ragged breath, she lifted her head and told herself to snap out of it.

Time for her to stop acting like some helpless female and take matters into her own hands.

The pep talk helped. She rose and splashed cold water on her face. Time to pull herself together. She knew something bad must have happened to Deputy Sean, so her best course of action would be to get to the FBI office in Knoxville. Granted, she was irked they hadn't returned her call, but maybe the person monitoring the calls didn't view this as a big enough emergency.

She hadn't seen any taxis driving around but believed Cooper when he said there was taxi service available. She could check with the nice man behind the counter, see if he could get a taxi to pick her up at the motel.

And Cooper too. Because as much as she wanted him to be safe, clearly these guys knew where he lived. That meant she'd need to get the FBI and the Marshals to offer him protection too.

At least until Frankie Germaine's men understood she was gone and Cooper wasn't a threat.

How to make that happen? She had no clue.

After using the facilities, she washed up again and opened the door. She almost walked right into Cooper who was hovering there.

His hands cupped her shoulders. "Mia? Are you all right?"

His concern for her welfare was touching, especially since he was the one who'd had to attack the guy lurking outside his apartment building.

"I'm fine." She tried to smile. "I'm more worried about you. How are your hands?"

He held her gaze. "They're fine. You're the one I'm concerned about. I'm sorry, Mia. I should have listened to you."

"Me?" She frowned. "What are you talking about?"

"You were the one who mentioned Junior's men may find out where I lived. We should have asked Chloe to drop us off here instead." As if realizing how that sounded, he quickly amended, "Or we should have just come here after she dropped us off rather than heading to my place."

"Please don't take this all on yourself." Tears threatened, and she held them off with an effort. "It's my fault really. I, uh, think it's better to concentrate on our next steps rather than second-guessing everything we could have done differently."

"You're right." Cooper released her but continued watching her with his incredibly intense gaze. "Let's try to get some sleep."

"Good idea." She edged around him and plopped onto the bed closest to the bathroom. His backpack was resting on top of the other bed. It was all they'd been able to take from his apartment, and she was glad she'd been able to hang on to it.

Sharing a room with Cooper seemed so intimate even though she knew he would continue to act like a gentleman.

It was her own overactive imagination that would get her into trouble.

Cooper disappeared into the bathroom. She kicked off her shoes, wincing at how painful her feet were, no thanks to their most recent trek through the city, and crawled into the bed fully dressed. Staring up at the ceiling, she tried to relax, but the images of their near miss with the man in the shadows flashed in her mind.

When she heard Cooper come out of the bathroom, she lifted up on her elbows. "I forgot to say thank you."

"For nearly getting you killed?"

She frowned. "No, for risking yourself to save me. This is crazy, Cooper. We have to stop running from these guys and find a way to get to the FBI. I can't believe they haven't called us back."

"I know." He sat on the edge of her bed. "We'll get out of the city first thing in the morning."

"It is morning," she said wryly.

That made him chuckle. "I know. But we can still get a couple hours of sleep." He leaned over and kissed her briefly before standing. "Hang in there, Mia. We'll get through this, together."

She was too choked up to do much more than nod. The guilt over how she'd dragged Cooper into danger was overwhelming.

Stupid tears leaked from the corners of her eyes, leeching down her face and dampening the pillow beneath her head. She squeezed her eyes closed and swallowed a sob.

Useless to cry over how she'd ruined Cooper's life. He'd made that initial choice, but she should have followed her instincts and slipped away before he became entangled in her mess.

Feeling desperate, she lifted her heart in prayer.

Loving God, we need Your strength and Your mercy more than ever. Please watch over Cooper to keep him safe from Frankie's men. You have blessed us so far with Your grace, please continue guiding us along Your chosen path. Amen.

It took a few minutes for the tension to ease from her body, for her tears to dry up. As impossible as it seemed, she must have fallen asleep because a noise outside their room woke her up.

Sunlight streamed through the narrow opening in the drapes covering most of the window. Voices could be heard as people moved by, likely discussing plans for the day.

Mia sat up, pushed her hair from her eyes, and peered at the clock. It was seven thirty, plenty of time yet before they needed to check out.

Cooper was still sleeping. Giving him the extra time he so badly needed, she slid out of bed, tried in vain to straighten her badly wrinkled clothes, and went into the bathroom.

After freshening up the best she could, she looked at her reflection and was surprised at the level of calm that washed over her. She shouldn't have been surprised, she'd always known God was with her.

Today she and Cooper would finally find the safety and security they deserved. And while she worried about Cooper's ability to return to Gatlinburg, she decided to leave everything in the Lord's hands.

Cooper was up and making coffee in the tiny machine

when she came out of the bathroom. "Just in time," he said with a grin. "I need to fill up the pot with water."

"Bathroom's all yours." She stepped aside to allow him to pass. "I think we should ask the guy behind the desk in the lobby to call us a cab."

"I agree." Cooper filled the coffee maker with water and pushed the button to brew. "We can take the coffee to go."

"Sounds like a plan."

Fifteen minutes later, they were ready. Obviously, not having luggage or a change of clothes meant they looked like refugees, but Mia did her best to ignore the fact that she looked and smelled bad.

Cooper opened the motel room door and took a moment to glance around before stepping outside. Mia followed, trying not to feel vulnerable as she closed the door behind her. They'd barely taken two steps toward the lobby when she caught a glimpse of a Gatlinburg police cruiser rolling by.

Divine intervention? She couldn't help but think this might be God's way of answering her prayers. She tugged on Cooper's knapsack. "Do you see the police car?"

He turned and nodded. "Let's go."

For a second, she remembered how she'd approached the squad sitting two blocks from her house after witnessing the murder of her father and stepmother. She shook off the memory and hurried over, waving her arms to get the officer's attention.

Seeing there was a female officer behind the wheel filled her with relief. The officer frowned, hit the brake, and rolled down the passenger side window.

"Is something wrong?"

"Yes. I was in witness protection, but my handler isn't answering his phone, and there are at least two men in black following me. Us," she amended as Cooper came up to stand beside her.

"WITSEC?" The officer looked surprised and suspicious. "Do you have any ID on you?"

"No, we've been on the run, and I was forced to toss my phone." Mia held the officer's gaze. "Please, you have to believe me. I need to get in touch with someone within the FBI. I left a message but haven't heard back."

"These are two sketches of the men who tried to grab Mia," Cooper added, showing her the drawings he'd made. "Unfortunately, the only distinguishing mark is the eyebrow scar on the one guy. I can verify we have seen these men at least three times in the past two days, and they are clearly looking for Mia."

The cop glanced from her to Cooper, then sighed. "Okay, give me a minute and I'll bring you into the station and hand you over to my boss. Lucky for you, this is Sergeant Kellen's weekend to work, and he's a good guy." She raised the window and spoke into her radio for several long seconds. Mia tried not to show her impatience as Cooper continuously swept his gaze over the area outside the motel.

The cop lowered the window again. "I've unlocked the back, go ahead and climb in."

This was a first for Mia, but she didn't hesitate. Cooper tossed his backpack in first, then slid in beside her. Mia tried to catch the officer's gaze in the rearview mirror. "Thank you for doing this."

The officer nodded and put the car in gear. "You could have come down to the station."

"We tried that, found the two men lurking nearby, so changed course," Cooper said in a matter-of-fact tone.

"Really?" The officer's eyebrows rose, nearly touching the brim of her hat.

"Yes." Mia attempted a smile. "It's been a harrowing couple of days."

The officer nodded but didn't say anything more. As they approached the police station, Mia glanced around hoping Frankie's men weren't out there waiting and watching. Not that they could get to her and Cooper while they were in the back of a police car, could they?

She hoped not.

The officer parked near the front of the building. She unlocked the back doors, then got out of the squad. Much like Cooper had done, the officer looked around before opening their door.

"Let's get you both inside," she said. When she saw Cooper's backpack, she frowned. "That will need to stay out here or searched for a weapon."

"You can search it," Cooper said. "It's mostly my art supplies."

"Okay, I'll take it then." The officer took the pack and led the way inside the building.

Once they were safely inside, Mia felt herself relax. This was it. Their nightmare was over. They were one step closer to actually talking to someone within the FBI.

The female officer's last name was Zurich, and she handed Cooper's backpack to the person sitting behind the desk. "This needs to be searched, and these two need to talk to Sergeant Kellen."

"He's in a meeting about the recent officer-involved shooting, but he should be out shortly." The woman behind the desk proceeded to search Cooper's pack. After several minutes, she closed it up and handed it back. "You're quite the artist."

"Thanks." Cooper shouldered the pack.

Fifteen minutes later, they were seated in the sergeant's office. Mia went through her story once again, this time explaining how she witnessed Frank Germaine Senior murdering her father and stepmother and that her handler had mentioned his son, Frankie Junior, was out for revenge. "I don't know exactly what Frankie looks like, I haven't had time to do a search for him on the computer."

Sergeant Kellen regarded them steadily for a long moment. "Okay, I'll make some calls, maybe I can get through where you couldn't. First, though, I have a meeting with my boss. We have a situation that needs immediate attention. The chief doesn't like to be kept waiting."

She swallowed hard. "Okay but try to make those calls as soon as possible."

The sergeant nodded and rose. "The minute I'm finished with the chief. In the meantime, I'll need both of you to sit and wait in one of our interview rooms. They're not comfortable, but it's the best I can do."

After exchanging a glance with Cooper, she nodded. "No problem, thanks." Mia rose and preceded Cooper out of the office and into the interview room.

"This could take longer than I thought." Cooper set his pack on the floor. "We should have asked for more coffee."

She grimaced and leaned back in her seat. "I've heard cop coffee is lousy."

"I'm willing to try it." He was sweet to try to lighten the mood.

"We need to find a way for you to be safe, Cooper. Those guys know where you live. We need the FBI or the Marshals to help relocate you."

He stiffened. "I like Gatlinburg."

She'd liked Chicago too. Well, most of the time. Not the

long winters, but the variety of seasons. Especially fall. "I know. I'm sorry."

He was silent for a moment. "Don't worry, we'll figure something out."

No one spoke for a long time. Mia stood and opened the door, intending to ask if she could go to the bathroom, when she heard a deep voice. "I'm from the US Marshals office. I understand you have our witness?"

She froze. No, this wasn't right. Sergeant Kellen hadn't made any phone calls yet. Unless the FBI had sent them? Her instincts were telling her it wasn't likely. Not without a return call. She grabbed Cooper's arm. "We have to get out of here. The front desk won't know they're not legit and may not believe us before it's too late."

Thankfully, he didn't argue. As Mia slipped out of the room, heading down the hall in the opposite direction from where the voice was located, she feared their chances of escaping the potentially fake marshal were slim to none.

CHAPTER TEN

When Cooper had overheard the guy introduce himself as a US Deputy Marshal, the hair on the back of his neck stood up. He didn't think it likely the FBI would send someone here without at least returning their call. Granted, they'd ditched Mia's phone, but they had his number. Getting out of the police station wouldn't be easy, but it might be better than wasting time trying to convince the cops that the marshal was fake.

If Junior's men had killed Sean, they'd have his badge, ID, and gun.

"Hey, where are you going?" Officer Zurich, the same woman who'd brought them in, walked toward them, her features etched in a deep frown.

"Is there a way out the back?" Cooper asked.

"Civilians aren't allowed here," Zurich insisted.

Mia grabbed her arm. "Listen, there's a guy back there claiming to be with the US Marshals office. He'll have a badge, ID, and gun, but I highly doubt he's for real. He likely killed the marshal and took his things. We need to get out of here, *now*!"

Zurich didn't look convinced. She shook off Mia's hand. "You sound paranoid. Why don't you sit down and I'll check this guy out? If he's fake, we'll arrest him."

"No time." Cooper dragged the sketches from his backpack and thrust them at her. "These are images of the two men who followed us and likely work for Frank Germaine Junior. Maybe one of these guys is the fake marshal and maybe not. But we're leaving."

Mia glanced frantically over her shoulder as if fearing the marshal was already coming toward them. "Please, Officer Zurich. I swear to you I'm not being paranoid."

Zurich's frown deepened as she reviewed the drawings, then she sighed. "I hope I don't lose my badge over this," she muttered. "Follow me."

Cooper fell in behind Mia as Zurich led them through a couple of hallways to the rear door of the police station. Above the door was a sign indicating an alarm would sound if the door was opened.

Mia stopped so abruptly he bumped into her. "What if the fake marshal hears the alarm?"

"Relax, there's a key code for us to use." Zurich punched in six digits, then opened the door. "See? No alarm."

"Thank you," Cooper said as Mia walked out into the sunshine. "We owe you one. I really hope you don't get into trouble for helping us."

Zurich shrugged, then thrust a business card into his hand. "Give me a call later, hopefully we'll get this straightened out."

He took the card but didn't make any promises. As much as he appreciated her offer, Zurich was a street cop working graveyard, he doubted she had much clout. Right now, his only goal was to get away from the police station without any of Junior's men finding them.

Gatlinburg was apparently too small of a city to successfully hide out in.

"This way," he urged, steering Mia through several parked squads toward the tree-lined area off to the right. It was the best place to find coverage.

But it was also the same place where one of Junior's men had hidden in wait.

For the first time in his life, he found himself silently praying. *Please, God, if You're listening, help us get out of here alive.*

They went from car to car until there was nothing else to use for cover. There was an empty ten yards or so between the last car and the tree line. As he and Mia crouched behind a squad, he cast a quick glance over the area.

No sign of Junior's men. He hoped they hadn't simply gotten better at hiding. He glanced at Mia. "Ready?"

She gave a jerky nod and abruptly rose and ran to the trees. He sprinted after her, and within minutes, they were hidden within the foliage.

He drew Mia down behind a large bush. "So far, so good."

"We can't stay," she protested. "The minute the fake marshal realizes we're gone, they'll be out here looking for us."

She was right about that, but they needed a plan. Some sort of destination. He worried the transit center would be too obvious. He tried to come up with an alternative location. "I say we take the trolley to Pigeon Forge. They'll have taxis there too."

Mia frowned, then nodded. "Okay. But I have no clue which trolley will take us there."

Cooper had to think for a minute. "I believe it's the pink route, takes tourists to Dollywood."

She looked confused, but there was no time to explain about the theme park named after Dolly Parton. "Okay, where do we find the pink trolley?"

"The route isn't that far from the restaurant where we ate lunch the other day." Looking back, it seemed like that was weeks ago rather than two days. He formulated a path in his mind. "Follow me."

Mia nodded. He rose and made his way through the small wooded area, coming out in a spot furthest from the police station. The hour was still early, so there weren't nearly enough tourists milling about to use as camouflage. Setting a brisk pace, he headed across the street and down two blocks to a large hotel.

Mia tugged on his arm. "Do you think the hotel has a shuttle bus?"

He hesitated, then shrugged. "I don't think so, most everyone gets around via the trolley. Come on, we need to keep moving."

As he was about to pass the hotel, he thought better of it and headed inside. Mia followed without saying a word. Knowing she trusted him to keep her safe steeled his resolve to make good on that promise.

Despite the stacked odds against them.

Rather than asking about a shuttle, he went through the lobby and down the hall. It had been a long time since he'd been inside the hotel, back in the days he and Trent used to steal from tourists, but thankfully it hadn't changed much. And he knew there was a side door leading to a parking lot.

Ignoring suspicious looks from a couple of staff

members, he quickly found the side door. Outside, he turned right toward the street.

"I feel so vulnerable out here," Mia whispered.

"Me too." He tried to smile reassuringly. "But we'll be okay once we get on that pink trolley."

He hoped.

They walked along the road for another hundred feet, then he took Mia down a narrow side street. He really wanted to stay off the main thoroughfares, but it wasn't easy to do.

Mia kept looking over her shoulder, and he couldn't blame her. He didn't think they'd been followed, but so far nothing had seemed to work.

How had Junior's men known they were at the police station anyway? He supposed it was possible they'd found the motel and had watched them get into the squad.

The only other alternative was that someone within the police station had tipped Junior's men off. And he honestly found that difficult to believe.

If there was someone working inside the police station, surely the cop could have picked them up by now, either on a trumped-up charge or pretending to have one of Junior's men in custody.

Still, this constant being on the run was getting old. It was one of the reasons he'd stopped stealing and turned to selling his art to make ends meet.

His heart ached for Mia and everything she'd been through. She'd been hiding from Junior for a couple of months now. And she should have been safe here.

"I see the sign for Serendipity up ahead." Mia's voice was breathless, so he slowed his pace a bit.

"Yes, we're very close," he assured her. "The trolley stop is just another couple of blocks from the restaurant."

A flash of disappointment darkened her eyes, but she didn't complain. He knew she was tired and sore from their long unplanned hike yesterday, and here they were putting more miles on today.

His feet weren't too happy about it either, but he tended to walk everywhere rather than riding the trolley, so he wasn't in as much pain as Mia. Hadn't she mentioned blisters on top of blisters? He felt bad for her, but they had to walk in order to stay hidden.

Normally, he walked to avoid being in close contact with strangers. A sensation that he hadn't once experienced with Mia. The thought was unsettling. Was this just because she was in danger?

No, he didn't think that was it. For some reason he was drawn to Mia, right from the very beginning. Even though she was going into a church, a building he'd always avoided.

And now? In the course of a handful of days, he couldn't stand the thought of her moving on without him.

He led her around the restaurant and to the side street that would take them to the pink trolley. A few more people were out and about now, probably those getting an early start on their trip to Dollywood.

Not his favorite destination, but in this case, a crowded trolley would be to their advantage. He slowed his pace more and took Mia's hand to make it seem like they were a tourist couple heading out for a day of fun.

Rather than running desperately for their lives.

Mia clung to his hand, making him long to pull her into his arms. Her honeysuckle scent teased his senses, but he told himself to stay focused. They weren't out of danger yet.

The pink trolley rolled to a stop about ten yards away. People surged forward to board in an attempt to secure one of the scenic spots located along each side of the trolley. He quickened his pace, trying to remember if he had exact change. The trolley fee was only a dollar, but they didn't give you change. He managed to find two singles in his meager stash. He and Mia stepped up and into the trolley. As before, he threaded through the travelers so that he and Mia were smack in the middle of the trolley.

He hung on to the pole with one hand, using the other to hold Mia close to his side. He wished they had their hats to help hide their faces but hoped their decision to head to Dollywood wouldn't be something Junior's men would anticipate.

If the bad guys did consider Pigeon Forge a viable location for them to go, they were in trouble. Because getting all the way to Pigeon Forge by trolley took far longer than simply driving by car.

Mia rested her head against his chest. "We're finally safe."

"Yeah." He pressed a kiss to the top of her head while thinking they were only safe for now.

Until the next curveball Junior's men tossed their way.

BEING CRADLED against Cooper helped give Mia strength, especially when he kissed the top of her head. Her feet felt as if they were on fire, so painful she wanted to cry, but she managed to swallow the lump in her throat and blink back her tears.

At least they were simply standing now rather than running. But she would have preferred sitting with her feet submerged in cold water. She inhaled Cooper's musky scent in an effort to distract herself from her various aches and pains. A flash of despair hit hard.

They should have been safe inside the police station. And it was disturbing to think that one of Frankie Germaine's men had managed to get Sean's badge, ID, and gun. Did the guy look similar to Sean too? Or was it possible that his ID wouldn't be looked at very closely? She could easily imagine that law enforcement types tended to stick together.

Yet she'd explained the truth to Sergeant Kellen who seemed to take her situation seriously.

Had they made the wrong decision to leave the police station? Doubts assailed her. There was a chance the FBI had sent a marshal to Gatlinburg. Without telling her? Maybe if they hadn't been able to reach her by phone. Yet, she couldn't deny the sense of urgency that had told her to get out.

She lifted her heart in prayer, knowing God was watching over them. Even if Cooper didn't believe that, she knew it to be true.

And here they were, both relatively unharmed and on their way to Dollywood. She couldn't imagine what a place with that name would be like, but she had sensed Cooper wasn't a fan. To her way of thinking, any place that was located far away from Frankie Germaine and his men was perfect.

The trolley lumbered at a slow pace. She lifted her head and glanced up at Cooper. "Does this thing go any faster?"

The corner of his mouth quirked up in a grin. "Nope. The scenic route is what people pay for."

Well, it was better than walking. "How long do you think it will take?"

He shrugged. "Forty-five minutes, an hour at the most."

It wasn't nearly as bad as she'd expected. "What's the plan once we get there?"

Cooper didn't answer right away. "Find a taxi, I guess." He sighed. "I don't know that much about the city, other than it sees more tourist traffic than Gatlinburg if you can believe it. Mostly because of people going into Dollywood. It's the main attraction."

"I see." She wondered if that was why he'd set up his sidewalk sketching in Gatlinburg instead. "I'm sure we'll find a taxi." She couldn't bear for this to be another dead end.

She found herself relaxing as the trolly headed through town. There were several different trolley lines, no way for Frankie's men to know for sure which one they were on.

Or if they'd taken a trolley at all.

"Maybe we should call Officer Zurich at some point," she said in a low voice. "See if the police believed the guy who showed up was really US Deputy Marshal Sean McCarthy."

"You really think the deputy is still alive?"

"Probably not. Although I ditched my phone yesterday, so he'd have no way of contacting me if he was."

"We'll try Officer Zurich later," he agreed. "She's probably heading home to get some sleep, considering she worked all night."

"You're right, it's probably better to wait." Mia told herself to be grateful the woman had helped them get away. If not for Officer Zurich believing in them, she and Cooper would have been escorted away by Frankie's men.

Maybe even Frankie himself.

The idea made her shiver.

She suddenly remembered something important. "Wait a minute, you gave your sketches of Frankie's men to Officer Zurich."

"I know, but I thought it might help in case one of those

two guys was the fake marshal, even though it's not likely. I mean, they surely would know we'd recognize them."

"Yeah, but I would have known the guy wasn't the real Sean anyway. Although maybe he was using another name. Either way, I was hoping we'd be able to give the sketches to the FBI." It probably wasn't the end of the world, but having the sketches helped give credence to her story.

She wanted to believe the FBI would believe her. There had to be records of how she'd witnessed the murder of her father and stepmother somewhere in the US Marshals files. All they'd have to do is make a few calls.

"Don't worry, I'll draw another set." Cooper smiled. "It will give me something productive to do."

She eyed him curiously. "You can do that after all this time has passed?"

"It's barely been two days, even though it seems much longer," he pointed out dryly. "Besides, I have a good eye for faces."

"I know, you do incredible work." She thought of the sketch he'd done of her. The black and white that was still tucked into the back pocket of her jeans.

Probably crumpled by now, but she didn't care. It was likely the only thing she had to remember him by.

She would have rather had a self-portrait of himself.

The trolley lurched to the side, sending her stumbling against him. She clung to Cooper's lean frame, thrilled with the way he held her close.

"I'm going to miss you, Cooper," she whispered.

He kissed her temple. "Same goes, Mia."

The way he held and kissed her was nice, but she longed for a real kiss. Logically, it didn't make sense, it wasn't as if they could have a relationship. Even if she could convince Cooper to enter witness protection, there was no guarantee the Marshals would let them to stay together.

Besides, Cooper had made it clear he liked living in Gatlinburg. Liked his life just the way it was, despite his incredible talent.

His choice, not hers. It would be wise to remember that.

The crowd around them on the trolley began to crane their necks and the level of chatter increased. Mia couldn't see over them to understand what had drawn their attention, but Cooper filled her in.

"Dollywood is just up ahead. We'll be stopping soon."

"Good news. Do you think we can grab something to eat?" The cup of coffee they'd had on the way to the police station was several hours ago.

"Yeah, there are plenty of restaurants," Cooper confirmed.

The trolley slowed as it approached its destination. A voice through the speakers warned the visitors that the last trolley ride back to Gatlinburg would be thirty minutes after Dollywood closed for the night. If they missed that trolley run, they'd have to wait until morning.

When the trolley finally stopped, Cooper hung back until everyone else had gotten off. When they were on solid ground, she gaped at their surroundings. "Good grief, it's a theme park on steroids."

Cooper chuckled. "You got that right. Which is why I don't like it here. Come on, let's find a restaurant."

The gaudy flashing lights and the screams from the people enjoying the rides were a twin assault on her senses. She reminded herself not to complain, the noise level didn't matter as long as they were safe.

As they strolled down toward a cluster of restaurants,

she glanced around for any sign of a taxi. Her spirits sank when she didn't find a single one.

"What do you think?" Cooper gestured to the restaurants. "Do you have a preference one way or the other?"

"Cheaper is better." She gestured toward the less crowded diner. "Let's try this one."

The interior of the diner didn't have the air-conditioning blasting at an intolerable level. Mia had found the summer months in Tennessee very hot and humid compared to Chicago.

Cooper found them a small booth. She sat with a low moan. "My feet are weeping with gratitude that we're sitting down."

"Mine too." Cooper pulled the plastic menu from the holder. "Looks like they have all the breakfast basics."

The prices were higher than she would have expected, but this was Dollywood after all.

They quickly placed their order. When they both had coffee, Mia sat back in the booth with a sigh. "It's nice to feel safe."

He eyed her over the rim of his mug. "We'll get a taxi to Knoxville from here."

"I didn't see any, but maybe they're hanging around in some central location." She sipped her coffee. "This hits the spot."

Cooper set down his mug and propped his elbows on the table. "It's eight thirty now. It's a little concerning we haven't heard back from the FBI, but we can stay somewhere close by for when they open on Monday. Hopefully, Sergeant Kellen followed through on those phone calls."

She nodded slowly. "I hope so too. Maybe his call will get someone to respond to ours."

He stared down at his mug for a long moment. "I'll get

you handed off to the FBI, but I'm not going to stay in Knoxville for very long. I need to get back to work."

His statement sent a chill down her spine. "Cooper, you can't just stroll back into Gatlinburg and pick up your life where you left off. Not until Frankie's men have been arrested. Or at the very least know that I'm out of reach because I'm safe with the US Marshals."

He raked an impatient hand through his hair. "I can try to hang around Knoxville for a while, but I can't just give up my life, Mia."

Can't? Or won't?

Frustrated with his stubbornness, she tried to come up with a way to sway him. Their food arrived, relatively quickly, and for that she was grateful.

"More coffee?" their server asked.

"Yes, please." Mia set her cup down for a refill.

Cooper did the same, then folded his hands and looked at her expectantly.

Her annoyance faded. She bowed her head and said, "Thank You, Lord, for guiding us safely out of Gatlinburg. We continue to ask that You grace us with the strength and courage we'll need to get to Knoxville. And we thank You for this food we are about to eat. Amen."

"Amen," Cooper murmured.

She reached over to touch his hand. "Thanks for joining my prayer."

The tip of his mouth curved into a reluctant smile. "I prayed for the first time in my life as we were escaping the police station. I want to believe God is watching over us, but it's not easy to get past the Preacher's lies."

"I believe in the devil, Cooper, and I have a feeling the Preacher is in hell where he belongs. Try not to dwell on the lies, and maybe at some point you'll attend a church service that will show you God's truth and God's light."

"Maybe." He didn't look interested in attending church. And she couldn't blame him. She honestly couldn't imagine the horror he and the other foster kids had endured over those years.

Although the fact that he'd prayed at all gave her hope that God was using this situation as a way to guide one of His lost children back home.

As much as Mia was honored to play an important role in the mission of bringing Cooper closer to God and faith, she still wished she could also convince him to stay away from Gatlinburg. Once she'd been relocated to a new city, in a new state, with a new US Deputy Marshal handler, she wanted, *needed* to know Cooper was safe.

She couldn't bear the thought of Cooper dying at the hands of Frankie's men solely because he'd come rushing to her rescue.

CHAPTER ELEVEN

Cooper had never before talked about praying or God to anyone. Not even to Trent.

Only to Mia.

It felt weird. He'd never attended church services. Yet Mia's faith seemed to have rubbed off on him. He couldn't help wondering if she was right about God's plan. God's light.

He viewed the time he and the others had spent with the Preacher as the dark years. Dark because of the abuse, dark because they'd been forced to sleep in the cellar. At times he felt as if there was a permanent dark stain on his soul. Was it possible God's light could counter that feeling? Maybe.

"Hey, it's okay. You don't have to attend church until you're ready," Mia said hastily. "I didn't mean to push."

"That might be never," he felt compelled to point out. He took another bite of his omelet. "But I have to admit that without church we wouldn't have met."

Her face lit up in a smile. "Exactly!"

After picking up his coffee mug, he eyed her across the table. "I really wish I had time to sketch you again."

"Again?" She wrinkled her nose and ate a piece of her toast. "You already sketched me twice. I don't think my face has changed since the last time."

It wasn't that, but he couldn't seem to put his feelings into words. "Your features are very expressive, and I've glimpsed many different nuances over the past few days. I haven't come close to capturing them all."

"Okay, now you're sounding a tad obsessive." Her smile indicated she was teasing. "And if you were going to sketch anything, you should do a second drawing of Frankie Germaine's men since we left the originals with Officer Zurich."

"I will." They wouldn't give his artist soul the same sense of satisfaction, but they would come in handy for when they finally made it to the Knoxville FBI office. And anything that would help ensure Mia's safety was important to him.

Their server arrived with their check and refilled their coffee. Cooper wished the meal could last forever, but of course, they needed to go. Finding a taxi driver willing to take them all the way to Knoxville might not be as easy as they'd hoped. Not to mention, the trip there and back would put a serious dent in his stash of cash.

Cooper told himself not to worry about next month's rent. He'd find a way to make it work. It wouldn't be the first time he'd cut back on groceries to the point of eating ramen noodles for dinner several nights a week.

Mia's safety was all that mattered.

As if she'd read his mind, she swooped on the bill. "It's my turn to pay."

Oddly enough, it bothered him to let her pick up the tab. Logically he knew it was foolish, but still, it rankled.

The real issue was that he wanted to spend more time with Mia. Her safety was key, but now that they were close to her final destination, he knew how much he'd miss her. If circumstances were different, he'd ask her to share a romantic dinner with him. To date her seriously and exclusively. Ironically, he now longed for the close intimacy he'd studiously avoided over the years.

Was this desperate need partially because he knew she was leaving? He didn't think so, yet he couldn't deny that his track record with relationships wasn't very good. Rachel, Chloe, Suzy, and several others were proof of that.

His fault, not theirs. He liked women, enjoyed spending time with them and sketching them. But he'd never let anyone touch his heart.

Until now.

Cooper went still as the realization sank deep. He cared about Mia, far more than he should. But they couldn't have a future, so he told himself to get over it and to finish his coffee. Mia set money on the table and rose. "I'm going to use the bathroom before we leave."

"Good idea." He'd do the same once she was finished.

Fifteen minutes later, they left the diner. The sun was hot, the humidity uncomfortably high, but Cooper didn't mind. He always preferred being outdoors. It was one of the reasons he'd chosen to sketch tourists for a living.

There were always server and kitchen job openings in the local restaurants. He'd tried that a few times, only to quit as soon as he had enough money to pay the rent.

Residual scars from his time with the Preacher? Maybe. It didn't really matter, he couldn't imagine changing his ways now.

"Which way do you think we should go?" Mia tucked a strand of hair behind her ear. "I'm not familiar with this city."

It had been a long time for him too, and he'd never tried to pick up a taxi here. "Let's check with the locals, they'd know the best place to find a taxi."

Mia glanced around, then gestured toward the front gate leading into the Dollywood theme park. "That guy should know."

She had a good point, so he nodded and headed back the way they'd come. As they walked, Cooper kept a wary eye out for any sign of Junior's guys. He didn't really think they'd been followed on the trolley, but double-checking his surroundings had become second nature.

Once they'd found a taxi, he figured he'd recreate his sketches on the drive to Knoxville.

The knot of dread in his gut wasn't easy to ignore. As they approached the Dollywood employee, he hung back as Mia smiled at him.

"Can you tell me where I can find a taxi to take me to Knoxville?"

The guy nodded. "Best place is near the trolley office located in Patriot Park." He waved a hand in the general direction. "You can't miss it." Then he frowned. "Gonna be expensive to get all the way to Knoxville."

"I know," she assured him. "Thanks for your help."

"We can probably grab a trolley to get to Patriot Park," Cooper told her.

"That might be best." She glanced down at her feet with a grimace. "My blisters are killing me."

"I know." He led the way over to the trolley stop. "We shouldn't have to wait long, they swing by every ten to fifteen minutes."

She nodded and glanced around. "I know we're safe here, but I can't seem to stop looking over my shoulder. I keep expecting one of Frankie's men to jump out at us."

"I'm afraid that feeling won't go away for a while." He slipped his arm around her waist and hugged her. "But it will get better, especially once you're settled in a new location."

"I hope so." She gazed up at him as if she wanted to say more but stopped as the trolley approached.

From the corner of his eye, he noticed a police car rolling slowly down the street. With a frown, he turned to look at it more closely.

It wasn't a Pigeon Forge cruiser. Instead, the words *Gatlinburg Police Department* could clearly be seen stenciled along the side.

Cooper turned his back and ducked his head, willing the trolley to hurry. In an effort to blend into the crowd, he eased closer to the other tourists waiting at the stop. Then he quickly shrugged out of his backpack, fearing it was too noticeable.

"What's wrong?" Mia whispered, sensing his tension.

"Hurry into the trolley." He subtly pushed forward, pulling Mia alongside him. He got a couple of dirty looks but ignored them. Once they were on the trolley, he tugged her down into one of the seats. "Keep your head down."

"Why? Who did you see?" Mia did as he asked, ducking low in her seat. "Frankie's men?"

"No, a Gatlinburg police cruiser." From their position inside the trolley, he couldn't see the squad anymore. But the fact that it was here at all worried him. It didn't make sense.

Mia frowned. "Did you recognize the driver?"

"No, unfortunately I didn't get a very good look at him."

He tried to pull the fragmented image to the forefront of his mind. "I'm pretty sure he wasn't one of the two men we've seen before."

Mia blanched. "You think he was the guy claiming to be a marshal?"

"Possibly." Cooper wished he'd gotten a better look at the guy. He hadn't paid much attention to the vehicle at all until he'd realized the squad was from Gatlinburg and not Pigeon Forge. "Although I would hope that after hearing your story, Sergeant Kellen would have already made his calls and arrested the man claiming to be a marshal."

"Maybe he left the police station before they could validate his credentials," Mia said in a low voice. "He could have used his credentials to flag down a squad, right?"

The thought was terrifying. "Yeah, he could have."

"You need to call Officer Zurich, see if she can shed any light on why a Gatlinburg police car would be in Pigeon Forge."

He hesitated, then nodded. Pulling his knapsack closer, he dug around for his phone and the card Zurich had given him. He noticed her first name was Felicia. He punched her phone number into his phone and listened to the ringing on the other side of the line.

Officer Zurich didn't answer, but at least it was her voice that invited him to leave a message. He spoke quickly. "This is Cooper and Mia, please give us a call back as soon as you can. We need to understand why we just saw a Gatlinburg police car in Pigeon Forge. We have reason to believe we may have been followed by the fake marshal."

After disconnecting from the call, there was a long silence.

"Maybe we're making a big deal out of nothing," Mia

said slowly. "It could be they share police duties between the two cities."

"They don't. Pigeon Forge has their own cops that patrol the city." He knew that as he'd dodged the police in those early days he and Trent had been stealing to survive. "Besides, it seems like a huge coincidence that we left the Gatlinburg police station through the back and hopped a trolley to Pigeon Forge only to have a squad from Gatlinburg show up."

Mia momentarily closed her eyes. "You're right, that is a pretty big coincidence."

Cooper didn't like the timing of the squad showing up. It was creepy, as if Junior's men had known exactly where they'd go. And he really wished he'd gotten a better look at the guy behind the wheel.

A legitimate cop? Or one of Junior's men? He had no way of knowing.

Unfortunately, he didn't think he could capture the guy's face in a sketch. He'd only gotten a fleeting glimpse at his profile, not seeing nearly enough of his features to draw his likeness.

A wave of frustration hit hard. Why did this keep happening? They should have been safe in Pigeon Forge.

They really needed to find that taxi to Knoxville ASAP.

The thought brought him up short. As the trolley slowed, he grabbed his pack and rose. "Come on, we're getting off."

"Here?" Mia looked around in surprise.

"Yeah." He took her hand. "Call me paranoid, but I'm worried the squad will look for us at the most logical place to get a taxi."

Mia didn't say anything as he led the way off the trolley. He didn't know the city of Pigeon Forge as well as he did

Gatlinburg, but if his memory served correctly, there was a very large hotel not far from here.

"I assume you have a destination in mind?" Mia said as he threaded his way through the crowd.

"Hopefully, the hotel valet will call a taxi for us." It was a long shot as he knew very well the employees catered to the hotel patrons, not bedraggled strangers strolling by seeking help.

But he sincerely hoped Mia could charm her way to getting a taxi. If there was any possibility their location was compromised, they needed to get out of Pigeon Forge in the next thirty minutes.

Before the mystery man driving the Gatlinburg police cruiser found them.

AS SHE STUMBLED AFTER COOPER, Mia clung to every ounce of self-control she possessed. She knew God was looking out for them, but hearing about a police car from Gatlinburg being in Pigeon Forge was worrisome.

Why was it that Frankie always seemed to be one step ahead of them?

It was all Mia could do not to drop to her knees and cry in despair. She tried to lift her heart in prayer, but it wasn't easy. Her feet were on fire, and every muscle in her body was sore and achy. Once again, she was tempted to simply give up. To let Frankie's men kill her and be done with it.

A wave of shame hit hard. No, giving up wasn't an option. Not for herself, and especially not for Cooper. She'd dragged him into danger, the least she could do was see it through.

For his sake as well as hers.

In fact, it could be that this latest turn of events would be enough to convince him to avoid Gatlinburg by staying in Knoxville for a while. The thought cheered her up.

As they turned the corner, Cooper abruptly stopped and turned. "This way."

Her heart thudded painfully in her chest as they skirted the corner and went down a street in the opposite direction from where they'd been going. What had happened? Had he seen the Gatlinburg police car again?

Cooper didn't give her an opportunity to ask. He moved so fast her feet screamed in protest.

"Please slow down." She tried not to let her face show her discomfort. "It's hard for me to keep up."

"Sorry." He glanced at her with concern. "I saw another police car but couldn't see enough to tell if it was local or from Gatlinburg."

"We can't run from every cop," she protested.

"Yes, we can. I refuse to trust the wrong person." His tone was flat and hard. "We tried the police department, remember? There's a smaller hotel this way, we'll ask the desk clerk for a phone number to call for a taxi. It's probably a better option than going to a large hotel."

She sighed, knowing she wasn't in a position to argue. After all, trusting Cooper's instincts, and her own, had gotten them this far.

Surely God wouldn't fail them now.

The motel was a step up from the place they'd spent the night. Mia pasted a smile on her face as they entered the lobby.

"Can I help you?" The young female clerk eyed them with a mixture of interest and wariness.

Cooper glanced at a rack of colorful brochures enumerating the various tourist activities and places Pigeon Forge had to offer. Estimating by the number of Dollywood pamphlets Mia could see from the center of the room, it was clearly the main attraction.

Mia approached the desk with what she hoped was an encouraging smile. "Do you have a phone number for the local taxi service? I really need to get back to Knoxville." She hesitated, then added, "There's been a death in the family." It wasn't in her nature to lie, but in her mind, Sean McCarthy was the only family she had left.

And she felt certain the poor guy had died in an effort to protect her.

"Oh, of course." Sympathy darkened the girl's eyes. "I have a number here, hang on a minute." The girl rummaged in a drawer. "They're all about the same price as far as going to Knoxville, it's the only method of public transportation to get there."

"I found that out the hard way." Mia took the card. "Thank you so much."

"Yes, we appreciate your help." Cooper had come up beside her. "Do you mind if we wait inside?"

The girl darted a glance over her shoulder and grimaced. "You'd better not, the manager will be back any minute, and he doesn't allow us to offer any amenities to non-guests."

"That's okay. We can wait outside. Thanks again." Mia subtly tugged Cooper's arm toward the door.

When they were back outside in the unrelenting sun, Cooper held out his hand. "Give me the card, I'll make the call. Unfortunately, I don't have much battery life left on this thing."

"What if the FBI tries to call us back?" she asked as she handed it over.

"I know that could be a problem. But at this point,

getting a taxi is our priority." He glanced at the number, then placed the call. "I need a taxi for two passengers to go to Knoxville please."

Mia couldn't hear what the other person said, but she noticed Cooper's expression turned resigned. "Thirty minutes? Nothing sooner?" Another pause, before he said, "Okay, that's fine. We're outside a place called The Forge Lodge."

"Thirty minutes, huh?" She glanced around searching for a place to sit. "It would be nice to find some shade."

"This way." Cooper lifted his chin toward the east. "There's a cluster of trees, and we should be close enough to see the taxi as it pulls in."

"Perfect." She followed him down and around the corner toward the trio of trees. She sank to the ground and leaned back against the tree trunk. "My feet will never be the same."

"Sorry about that." Cooper eased off his pack, then dropped down beside her. "I'll admit my feet are sore too."

They were silent for several minutes before she turned to him. "Cooper, will you please consider staying in Knoxville for a while?"

He sighed heavily. "Nah. The FBI will help you out, Mia. They're not going to be interested in me."

"You don't know that." She was encouraged that he hadn't outright refused. "Once you show them your sketches, I believe they'll agree you need just as much protection as I do."

He was quiet for a long moment. "I'm not interested in leaving Gatlinburg to be relocated somewhere else."

The pang of hurt was difficult to ignore. "Not even for my peace of mind?"

He stared out toward the road where throngs of tourists

moved from one attraction to the next. "This is my home, the only place my foster brother Trent knows where to find me."

She frowned. "Where is Trent now? Didn't you already leave him a message?"

He turned to look at her. "I thought once you went into WITSEC, you had to leave everyone behind."

She flushed and glanced away. "Yes, that's true. But you could stay in Knoxville for a while without going into WITSEC."

"Maybe. But chances are good that Junior's men will manage to find me as it's not easy to hide when I'm sketching for tourists."

"You could take a different job temporarily." Honestly, she was getting annoyed with him. He acted as if sketching was his only option when, in fact, he could easily get any number of jobs.

Something far less noticeable than sidewalk sketching.

"No, I can't." His curt tone held a note of finality. "Give it up, Mia. You can't change who I am."

That was true. Cooper was the only one who could do that. And clearly he had no desire to do any such thing.

She swallowed her frustration and stared out at the street as if searching for their taxi. Yet every cell in her body was tuned to Cooper.

He sat motionless as if braced for her to offer additional arguments. The silence was deafening, and the minutes dragged by with excruciating slowness.

Cooper abruptly pulled out his sketchbook and began drawing. She watched as he recreated the two men Frankie Germaine had sent after her.

When Cooper's phone rang, he was so startled he dropped his chalk.

"Who's calling?" She frowned as she tried to see the screen.

He hesitated. "I don't recognize the number."

"It's not Officer Zurich's cell or Trent's? Or the FBI?"

"Nope." He set the phone aside. "It's a Gatlinburg area code."

"Tell me about Trent."

Cooper shot a glance at her. "He's the same age as I am and currently lives in Nashville."

"How long has it been since you've seen him?"

"Over three years." He finished the first sketch and moved onto the next. "Trent plays guitar for the Jimmy Woodrow Band. Last I heard they've been doing fairly well."

"I see." Although she really didn't. "If you haven't seen him in a while, why do you feel the need to stay in Gatlinburg?"

"I told you, it's my home." The edge was back in his tone.

"What about your other foster siblings? Have you seen any of them recently?"

"No." His phone rang again. He picked it up with a frown. "It's the same number."

"Just answer it already." She was losing her patience with him. Stubborn man. "If it's spam, you can hang up."

He lifted the device to his ear. "Hello?" In a heartbeat, he set the sketch aside and glanced at Mia. "Hang on, I'm going to put you on speaker." He pushed a button and held the phone between them. "You're calling from the police station?"

"Yes, Sarge called me back in. He wanted to know why I helped you two leave the police station." Mia recognized Officer Zurich's voice.

"Hang on, I'm going to call you back." Cooper abruptly ended the call.

Mia gaped at him. "What are you doing?"

He shook his head and stared down at the phone. "I know it sounds paranoid, but I left her a message on her cell phone. Why didn't she call me back using that number instead?"

"Because she's at work?" Mia wondered if the sun was getting to him.

He shook his head and pushed a button on the phone. Then he held it out so she could hear too. It didn't take long for Officer Zurich to answer. "Cooper, what is wrong with you?"

"I'm not going to apologize for double-checking you are in fact at work." Cooper's tone was testy. "And you better make this fast, my phone is running out of juice."

"I put my job on the line for you two," Officer Zurich said irritably. "Do you want to hear what I know or not?"

"Yes, we do," Mia quickly interjected.

"Listen, I spoke to Sarge at length about your concerns about the marshal. Sounds like the minute the guy claiming to be the US Marshal heard you two were no longer in the building he stormed out."

"Go on," Cooper encouraged. "Have you issued an arrest warrant for the guy?"

"We have, but that's not the main reason I called," Officer Zurich continued. "Sarge took the two sketches you gave me and sent copies to every squad in the city."

"That's great news," Mia said. "I'm sure those men were hired by Frankie Germaine."

"You need to have the cops check out the trolley station," Cooper added. "Oh, and you should know I caught a glimpse of a Gatlinburg police car here in Pigeon Forge."

"Are you sure about that?" Officer Zurich sounded shocked by the news.

"Absolutely positive. I saw the Gatlinburg stenciled along the side of the cruiser. Unfortunately, I didn't get a clear look at the driver."

"That's not good," she muttered. "Pigeon Forge is not our jurisdiction, there would be no reason for one of our cops to drive there."

"Yeah, well, someone is here," Cooper insisted.

"I need to let Sarge know about that," she said on a sigh. "But listen, the main reason I called was to tell you we need you both to come back to Gatlinburg."

"No way." Cooper's refusal was knee-jerk. "Those guys are still searching for us."

"I agree with Cooper," Mia added. "It's too dangerous. We have a taxi on the way, and our next stop will be Knoxville."

"You don't understand, we have the two men Cooper sketched in custody," Officer Zurich said. "We need you both to identify them as the men who tried to assault you."

Mia stared at Cooper for a long moment. It was good news to learn Frankie's men were in custody, but was it safe to return to Gatlinburg?

What if the fake marshal was hiding nearby, waiting for them?

CHAPTER TWELVE

"Cooper? Mia? Are you still there?" Officer Zurich's voice drifted up from the speaker on his phone.

Cooper cleared his throat. "Yeah, we're here. But I'm not sure returning to Gatlinburg is a good idea. Mia needs to be safe."

"If you don't come here to identify them and press charges, these guys could walk," Zurich warned.

"We're coming, don't worry," Mia quickly spoke up. "Do not let those men go. I know they're working for Frankie Germaine."

"Yeah, well, they claim they have no idea who he is," Officer Zurich said wryly. "Sergeant Kellen really wants to talk to both of you."

"Yeah, well, let's hope he can keep us safe then," Cooper said, irritated by Mia's willingness to simply return to Gatlinburg. "Because we've been running from danger for days now, and it's getting old."

"Understood. I need to let Sarge know about the Gatlinburg squad you've seen in Pigeon Forge too. That's definitely unusual." Officer Zurich hesitated, then asked, "Do you want me to come pick you up in a squad? Or I can use my personal vehicle if that makes you feel better."

He considered that option for a moment. Being picked up in her personal vehicle would be nice, yet it would take her a while to get here. When he saw their taxi heading toward them, he made a quick decision. "No need, we have a ride, thanks."

"Okay, call me when you get here," Zurich said.

"We will." He ended the call and shut down the phone to preserve the small amount of battery he had left. Then he glanced at Mia. "Are you sure about this? There's still time to change your mind. The taxi is already prepared to take us to Knoxville. We can always call Officer Zurich from there."

"We can't let those men go, Cooper." Mia's gaze was pleading. "We need them locked up behind bars. They might give up key information on Frankie to save themselves."

"And what if they don't?" Cooper tucked his phone in his backpack and shouldered it as the taxi drew closer. "We'll be taking a risk for nothing."

"We're taking a risk to do the right thing," Mia countered. "It's our civic duty to keep criminals off the streets. Besides, if they're locked up, they can't hurt us anymore."

"Whoever masqueraded as a US Marshal is still on the loose," he protested.

"And I'm sure the police will find him."

He wasn't convinced the Gatlinburg police would find the fake marshal, but she was right about doing their civic duty. However, that didn't make it any easier to comply with her wishes. In that moment, Cooper realized he'd gone through the past few years thinking only of himself. It hadn't occurred to him how selfish that was until now.

"Besides, the FBI office is closed, right? They won't be

open until tomorrow morning. We may as well see if Sergeant Kellen has better luck getting through to the Feds."

He couldn't deny her logic. As he approached the taxi, the driver lowered the passenger window. "Change of plan, we need to head back to Gatlinburg instead of Knoxville."

The driver looked annoyed but gestured with his hand. "Fine, get in."

Cooper opened the back door for Mia, then tossed his knapsack inside and joined her in the back seat. The interior was hot and stuffy as if the cabbie's air-conditioning was broken. Or maybe the guy was too cheap to run it.

The driver named his price, which was half of what it would have cost to get to Knoxville. Seemed expensive, but they weren't in a position to negotiate. When they agreed to pay the fee, the driver merged into traffic, heading back the way they'd come.

He watched out the back window for a bit, making sure the squad from Gatlinburg wasn't following them. Or anyone else for that matter.

"Thanks for doing this, Cooper." Mia kept her voice low.

"No reason to thank me. As you said, these guys need to remain behind bars." As much as he wanted to get Mia out of danger once and for all, there was a tiny, selfish part of him that was relieved to have the ability to spend more time with her.

Even a couple of hours was better than nothing. And yeah, he could secretly admit that sounded crazy. As if a few more hours would hold him over for the rest of his life.

He thought about how Mia had begged him to stay in Knoxville. The idea had tempted him more than he wanted to acknowledge. In the end, though, he knew Mia wouldn't be sticking around Knoxville.

No, the US Deputy Marshals would whisk her off to a new city in a new state, likely far away from Tennessee. Maybe even on the west coast.

He'd never been to the ocean. Had only been in Asheville, North Carolina, and then Cherokee where the Preacher's cabin was located. After escaping the fire, he, Trent, and Sawyer had moved through the Smoky Mountains, ending up in Tennessee.

What had happened to them? Sawyer, Hailey, Darby, Jayme, and little Caitlyn. They'd split up heading off in different directions to minimize the probability of getting caught by the authorities. They'd all unanimously agreed to never go back into the system.

He and Trent had hung with Sawyer for a while, but at the time, Sawyer was bossy, and he and Trent had decided they were better off on their own.

A decision he regretted now.

But going somewhere else? Permanently living in a strange place? He honestly couldn't imagine it.

"Cooper?" Mia reached out to take his hand. "We're going to be okay."

"I hope so." He forced a smile and was glad the driver was listening to music rather than paying attention to them. "At least Officer Zurich believes us."

"I'm sure Sergeant Kellen does too. We just need to get in touch with the FBI."

He gently squeezed her hand. "I'm sure he'll fill us in when we get there."

She nodded, her expression troubled. "It seems like we've been on the run for weeks rather than a few days."

"I know. But as you said, it's because you chose to do the right thing."

"My father and stepmother were murdered." She shivered. "I know God has a plan, but it's not always easy to accept His will."

He didn't know much about God's plan. Was it possible God intended for him to notice Mia coming and going from the church? To have him follow her and to prevent Junior's men from kidnapping and killing her?

He could see that God would want to protect Mia, she was one of His children. But why involve him? A guy who'd shunned God and the church and everything the Preacher claimed to stand for?

Or maybe because of it.

He gave himself a mental shake. This type of internal philosophizing wasn't like him. He preferred dealing in reality. Sketching for tourists and living a quiet life.

A boring existence.

Cooper glanced out the rear window again, noting the taxi driver was nodding along with the music, making good time in getting them back to Gatlinburg. The trolley had been slow and scenic, while the taxi ate up the miles in what seemed like record time.

Once they hit the city limits, Cooper leaned forward. "We need to go to the police station."

"I don't know where that is," the driver said, meeting his gaze in the rearview mirror.

"I'll give you directions. It's not far." Ironic that Cooper knew all about getting to the police station, considering he'd spent the past thirteen years of his life avoiding the authorities.

Ten minutes later, the taxi driver pulled up in front of the police station. Cooper dug out his phone and turned it on. He called Officer Zurich. "We're here, meet us out front."

"O—" The phone went dead. That was it for what was left of his battery.

He shoved the useless phone back into his pocket. He paid the driver, trying not to wince at how they were blowing through cash. All for a good cause, but it was still concerning. Especially considering he hadn't worked in several days. Weekends were peak tourist times, and he'd blown this one off.

When Officer Zurich emerged from the building, he waited until she was close before pushing his door open. He helped Mia out, using his body and his knapsack as a shield. "Let's get her inside."

"Sarge is waiting." Zurich took the position behind them as they headed into the police station.

Sergeant Kellen was indeed standing in the lobby area. "Thanks for coming in."

"We would have stayed, if that guy claiming to be with the US Marshals Service hadn't come looking for us." Cooper held the sergeant's gaze. "We knew you hadn't had time to make the phone calls to the FBI yet."

Kellen looked pained. "I know, I should have put the front desk on alert right away. I wasn't expecting anyone to walk in like that. And the way he quickly disappeared did raise the clerk's suspicions, even though his credentials were real, but by then it was too late."

"Yeah, likely stolen from a dead marshal." Cooper felt Mia's hand on his arm and tried to dial back his frustration. He wasn't happy to hear the fake marshal was still on the loose. "I hear you have suspects in custody."

"We do." Kellen inclined his head. "Please come this way."

As before, Cooper was required to have his bag searched. "It's no different from the last time you looked," he protested.

"Standard protocol," the woman countered.

"It's for everyone's safety," Mia added.

Yeah, he imagined this woman would be extra vigilant after the goof up with the fake marshal. When the woman finished searching his bag, he slung it over his shoulder and followed Sergeant Kellen down the hall. He stopped and gestured to an interview room, the same one they were in before.

"Please have a seat," Kellen said. "We have a couple of photo arrays to show you."

"No lineup?" Cooper asked.

"Easier for us to find mug shots to use as a comparison rather than searching around the city for actual people," Kellen informed them. "Tends to put a damper on the tourist crowd if we approach them for this kind of thing."

"I can imagine." Cooper pulled out his phone and charger, then tucked his pack beneath the table and sat beside Mia. "I need to charge my phone while we're here. We're waiting on a call from the FBI."

"Go ahead. I'm going to ask you to each review the photo array separately," Sergeant Kellen said. "Cooper, please move to the opposite end of the table."

He could understand the need for each of them to make their own ID without help from the other, but he didn't like leaving Mia's side. Still, he did as Kellen requested.

The sergeant stood and put two sheets of paper in front of Mia, then moved down to hand him two as well. It took him less than a minute to pick out the two men he'd drawn.

"This guy and this one." He tapped the images, one on each paper.

"Thanks." Kellen picked up the papers, then moved over to where Mia was still studying the faces.

"This guy, here," she said, pointing at one. "And this one too."

"Excellent, thank you." Sergeant Kellen nodded in satisfaction. "You both picked the two suspects we have in custody."

"I'm glad to hear that." Mia leaned back in her chair, sighing with relief. "They'll stay in jail now, right?"

Kellen hesitated. "I believe you both, but you need to understand their story is that you attacked them, Cooper."

"Two against one," he shot back. He moved closer to Mia. "And this guy"—he pointed to the image of the second man—"grabbed Mia's arm and tried to pull her along with him."

"I know, I have Mia's original statement." Kellen glanced at them. "But you just need to know what you're up against."

"Have you run their fingerprints through the system?" Mia leaned forward, pinning the sergeant with her gaze. "Because I believe these guys were hired by Frankie Germaine Junior. He probably blames me for his father, Frank Germaine Senior, being convicted of murdering my father and stepmother."

"I did, so far nothing popped. I just heard back from the FBI, they finally returned my call." Kellen paused for a long moment, then said, "Two things you need to know. One is that US Deputy Marshal Sean McCarthy is dead. The other is that Frank Germaine Senior is also dead."

"I suspected Sean, but Frank Senior is dead?" Mia's mouth dropped open in stunned surprise. "How? Why? What happened?"

Kellen shook his head. "The Feds haven't coughed up

any pertinent details. Other than they wanted you to know, Mia. And they're sending someone to pick you up."

Cooper glanced at Mia, who still looked shell-shocked. "No wonder Frankie is out to kill me."

"We believe Frankie is out to kill both of you," Kellen corrected.

"Me?" Cooper wasn't buying that.

"Yeah, you." Kellen held Cooper's gaze. "Think about it. You fought the two idiots and got the better of them, and you also helped Mia escape."

It was Cooper's turn to sit back in his chair in stunned silence. Mia had claimed he was in danger, but he hadn't wanted to believe it.

Now, Kellen was telling him the same thing.

Beads of sweat popped out on his forehead. Cooper didn't want to be stuck inside some sort of safe house. He didn't want to be relocated somewhere new.

What had he done?

———

MIA NOTICED the flash of panic in Cooper's expression and felt terrible for dragging him into the middle of her problems.

He'd chosen to help protect her, but after that, it was all on her. She never should have stayed in his apartment. Never gone to lunch with him.

She never ever should have let things get this far.

Now it seemed as though Frankie had a price on both of their heads. And even with the two men being in custody, she was very much afraid others would follow.

Unknown men whom they'd never recognize, until it was too late.

She sent up a silent prayer for Sean McCarthy. She felt bad that the US Marshal had died protecting her.

So much death. So much hate. She couldn't wrap her mind around it.

The silence lengthened until she asked, "When exactly will the FBI get here?"

"Soon," Sergeant Kellen said. "I just spoke to them, they asked us to keep you both here so that you're safe."

"What about the fake marshal?" Cooper asked. "Have you found him yet?"

"No. Although we did ask Wanda, our front desk clerk, to work with a sketch artist." Kellen lifted a brow. "You want to see it when it's finished?"

"Yes," Mia said.

"I'm more interested in having the sketch sent to the FBI," Cooper countered. "He's very likely to be another of Junior's known associates."

"That's been done," Kellen confirmed. "Understand it's Sunday, so they're scrambling a bit. I'm sure we'll get an update when they arrive."

Cooper narrowed his gaze. "I should hope so."

The sergeant grimaced. "I'll call and ask that they bring what they have. In the meantime, make yourselves comfortable." Kellen left the room, taking his photo array of suspects with him.

"I don't like this," Cooper muttered.

"I'm sorry." Mia reached out to take his hand. "I know this is my fault, and I wish I would have handled things differently. But honestly, this is for the best. I would have worried about you staying in Gatlinburg."

Cooper's expression went tight, and his breathing looked ragged. Mia wondered if being in the cellar had given him claustrophobia. "That may be, but I'm not leaving."

She tightened her grip on his hand. "I know you're scared, I felt the same way when I had to leave Chicago."

"That's the first time you mentioned Chicago." He frowned. "You're a long way from there."

"Trust me, I'm very aware of that." She held his gaze. "Cooper, I know how hard this is for you, but you can't stay here. Not until Frankie Germaine has been arrested."

"And when will that be?" His voice rose in agitation. "Weeks? Months? Years?"

"I don't know."

He pulled away, rose to his feet, and began to pace. She could tell he was struggling with the idea of going into witness protection. Giving up your life, your name wasn't easy. Yet Cooper didn't have the same sort of community ties that she'd had.

"I'm not going." Cooper's tone was flat and hard.

As much as she empathized with him, she didn't really understand why he was so resistant. "Why is this so difficult for you?" she asked. "You live here alone and told me you haven't seen Trent in three years."

"I don't like being told what to do." He blew out a breath and raked his hand through his hair. "That made me sound like a bratty kid, but here's the thing. Gatlinburg is where Trent knows he can find me. I spoke to him last a year ago, what if he wants to come back? This is the place that I've called home for the past several years. I have no interest in leaving."

"I know it's not easy. Going into WITSEC means giving up your family and friends." Mia's voice was low. "My family was dead, but I gave up a lot of friendships. People who are probably wondering where I am."

"I know you think I'm being a stubborn idiot. But I can't give up my art, Mia. Sketching for tourists is the only way I know how to earn a living."

"You're talented enough to do more than tourist sketching," she said automatically. Then grimaced. "Although, you are right. The US Marshals wouldn't want you to have anything to do with art once you've been relocated to your new home."

"It would be easier to cut off my arm." He turned and stared at the walls of the interrogation room. After what seemed like an eternity, he finally turned to face her. "I can't do it. I'd rather take my chances with Junior's men."

She gaped at him. "You don't mean that."

"I do." He reached down and snagged his pack and pulled his phone and cord from the wall. "This isn't how I wanted things to end, Mia. I care about you, more than anyone else. But I can't give up my life."

"Cooper, please, don't leave." Mia jumped up and planted herself in front of the door. "At least give the authorities some time to find Frankie and his men."

"There's no point in waiting." He stepped forward, frowning when she didn't retreat. "Mia, if you care about me at all, you'll let me go."

Tears welled in her eyes. "I do care about you, Cooper. That's why I'm begging you to stay."

"I'm sorry. I don't want to hurt you, Mia, but I won't survive without my art." He reached for the door handle.

"Please, Cooper." She threw herself into his arms. He gathered her close, and she clung to him, wishing she could find a way to convince him to stay with her.

To share his life with her.

Deep down, she knew once she let him go, she'd never see him again.

HURTING Mia was akin to hurting himself. Cooper hated making her cry, but he also couldn't find the strength to let her go. Instead, he gathered her close, inhaled her honeysuckle scent, and wished more than anything things could be different.

That he could be the man she needed.

"Cooper." Her voice was muffled against his shirt. When she lifted her head, he couldn't find the willpower to resist the urge to kiss her.

Her mouth eagerly clung to his, need and desire seeming to fuse them together into one. Their kiss was so intense his resolve wavered.

Could he really give up Mia? It seemed about as impossible as giving up his art.

He broke off the kiss, breathing heavily as his thoughts whirled. Sure, he could try to start over someplace new. But doing that, giving up life as he knew it, would likely end up in his feelings toward Mia turning quickly into resentment.

Which wouldn't be fair to either of them.

"I'm sorry." His voice was low and rough. "I have to go."

Mia turned away and sank back into her seat. He opened the door and looked back at her, searching for something to say.

But he couldn't force the words past his tight throat.

I love you.

The words echoed in his mind as he turned and headed out of the interrogation room. He couldn't seem to breathe normally until he was all the way outside. He stood with his face to the sun for a long moment before the tension eased from his body.

He relaxed, even though the ache in his heart remained.

Resisting the urge to look back over his shoulder, he set out walking.

Leaving Mia was difficult, and he knew danger still lurked nearby. The two men who'd attacked Mia had been put in jail, but he understood there could be others.

Especially the fake marshal.

But really, how would any of Junior's men know how to find him? Mia had testified against Senior, but he'd only been involved with the two men who were currently being held by the Gatlinburg police. It was possible the two guys had mentioned he was an artist, but he wasn't the only artist in the area.

There was another artist, a woman about ten years older than him, who sold her art on the street. She didn't sketch people the way he did but worked in oil creating beautiful landscapes. Not that he wanted her to be in danger, but there were also several art shops scattered around Gatlinburg too.

Rather than heading back to his apartment, Cooper decided to head downtown to work for a while. It was time to make up for taking the past few days off. And he had his art supplies, so no need to go back to the apartment.

The place would seem empty now that Mia was gone. Steeling his resolve, he continued walking while keeping a wary eye out for anything suspicious.

He could always call Officer Zurich if he needed something. Huh. First time in his life he'd ever considered a cop as someone who could help.

The area where he normally worked was crowded with tourists. Without wasting a moment, he unpacked his easel and set up a fresh piece of paper. Some of his charcoals were broken, likely from when Mia had used his backpack as a weapon, but he told himself to get over it. Charcoals were easily replaced.

Mia wasn't.

When he sat down on his collapsible stool, he glanced beyond his easel and saw the church. People were streaming out of the place after attending Sunday services.

He had to swallow against the hard lump that had formed in his throat. Was this how it would be? Seeing Mia everywhere he turned? Remembering every moment of the time they'd spent together?

Their kisses?

"I see you're back."

The woman's caustic tone drew his attention. It was the same tourist who'd approached him the day he'd taken off after Mia. It took far more willpower than he thought possible to drum up the enthusiasm to sketch her.

"Yes, I'm so sorry I had to run off like that. I learned of a death in the family." He didn't have to act bereaved, leaving Mia behind had felt like losing a part of himself. "Please accept my sincere apology."

"Oh, I'm sorry to hear that." The woman's demeanor changed from irritated to sympathetic. "No wonder you've been gone the past few days."

"Yes." He didn't elaborate but picked up one of his charcoals. "Would you care to sit? A beautiful woman like you deserves to be put to paper."

"I'd like that." She didn't hesitate to seat herself on his second collapsible stool.

She kept up a series of comments about the town as he worked. Again, Cooper couldn't believe how difficult it was to stay on task. Several times he wanted to tell her to be quiet, but of course, he managed to refrain.

He finally finished the sketch, not his finest work but not terrible. And he'd drawn her in a very positive light.

"It's beautiful," she gushed, pressing four twenty-dollar bills into his hand. "Thank you."

"You're welcome." He almost told her to send her friends when he caught a glimpse of a dark-haired woman out of the corner of his eye coming out of the church. At first he thought of Mia, but the woman's hair was straight rather than wavy, her face more oval than heart-shaped. There was something familiar about her . . .

"Cooper? Is that you?" The woman crossed the street and strode toward him, a tall guy at her side. He finally recognized her as his foster sister.

"Hailey? How did you know I was here?" He stepped forward to greet her with a hug. "Did you come all the way to Gatlinburg just to attend church?"

"No, silly, I've been living in Gatlinburg for five years, but I rarely come into town. In fact, I avoided coming here until the past few weeks." She eyed him critically. "Cooper, I can't believe it's you. That I found you after all this time. I found Sawyer and Darby, too, they're both going to be thrilled to know you're here. Where is Trent, by the way?" Then she looked embarrassed and tugged the tall man closer. "Oh, I'm sorry. This is my fiancé, Rock Wilson."

Hailey lived in Gatlinburg? Had met up with some of the fosters? Was engaged? And went to church? His mind spun crazily, there was so much he wanted to know, especially about the other foster kids. But then he caught sight of Mia coming toward them. He frowned with concern, stepping forward to meet up with her. "Mia, what are you doing here?"

"Looking for you." Mia crossed her arms over her chest

as she looked at Hailey. "Is she another one of your girl-friends? Or someone looking for a sketch?"

"Neither, she's my foster sister." He ignored Hailey's amused smile. "But, Mia, you shouldn't be out in the open like this." He drew her closer to where Hailey and Rock were watching with amusement. "Hailey, Rock, this is Mia. Mia, my foster sister, Hailey and her fiancé, Rock."

"Nice to meet you." Hailey offered her hand.

"Nice to meet you too." Mia glanced at Cooper. "He mentioned his foster siblings but not that you lived in the area."

"I had no idea Hailey lived here." Cooper cast a quick glance around. "Mia, it's dangerous for you to be here like this. You need to get back to the police station."

"Yeah, I do." Mia surprised him by turning away. "Goodbye, Cooper."

As quickly as she'd arrived, Mia was gone. He noticed she met up with Officer Zurich who drew Mia toward a squad parked nearby.

"What was that about?" Hailey asked. "Why is she in danger?"

Cooper shook his head helplessly. "It's a long story."

"We have plenty of time," Hailey said.

He nodded but wasn't really paying attention. Watching Mia walk away was even more difficult the second time around.

CHAPTER THIRTEEN

Cooper had reunited with his foster sister who lived in Gatlinburg.

Mia had hoped to try one more time to convince him to come along with her. Had asked for Felicia's help to drive her there. Mia had been full of hope, until Cooper and Hailey had embraced. The beautiful dark-haired girl was Hailey. His sister. His family.

Cooper and his foster siblings had been through a lot together. They'd survived and thrived, despite the horrors they'd suffered while living with the Preacher. How fair would it be to ask Cooper to leave Hailey and Trent behind so soon after finding them?

Not that anyone ever promised life would be fair. Because it wasn't.

She knew that better than anyone.

"Mia? Are you okay?" Felicia's voice was full of sympathy.

"Yeah." No, she wasn't fine. Her heart ached for what she'd lost, but Mia reminded herself that she was following

God's plan. Not her own. And really, Cooper had made up his mind to stay even before learning about Hailey. Finding Hailey had likely sealed the deal.

Mia knew he'd cared about her. But she also knew Cooper didn't love her.

Not the way she'd fallen in love with him.

"Let's head back to the precinct." She tried to smile. "The FBI will be arriving soon."

"Okay." Felicia smiled sadly. "I'm really sorry things didn't work out."

"Me too." Ironic that Mia had found two friends in Gatlinburg, Felicia and Cooper, but only after her WITSEC cover had been blown.

Friends she would once again be forced to leave behind.

Enough already. There was no point in wallowing in self-pity. She absolutely needed to put her faith in God and pray that Frankie Germaine was found by the police sooner rather than later.

The sketch Wanda had done hadn't been detailed enough for her to recognize the man pretending to be Sean. She had not met Frankie Junior face-to-face, although she'd heard he resembled his father. Yet it was more likely the sketch was of someone Frankie had hired.

Hence the requirement to relocate her to a new city and state.

Starting over, again.

Felicia managed to get them back to the police station without running into trouble. Mia waited for the officer to open her door for her before hurrying inside. Sergeant Kellen scowled at them. "You shouldn't have left the building."

"It's my fault," Mia spoke up quickly. "Officer Zurich

didn't want me to go, but I insisted. She followed to make sure I was okay. And as you can see, I'm fine."

"You and Cooper are giving me gray hair," he muttered. "I just heard from the FBI, they're going to send a new US Marshal who will take you into custody, instead of coming themselves."

Mia frowned. "Why would they do that?"

"I don't know." Kellen's tone was testy. "The federal government didn't see fit to fill in a measly local cop, despite the stripes on my sleeve. Regardless, it looks like you'll be our guest for a while longer."

"Okay." The situation wasn't ideal, but there was nothing she could do about it. It made her nervous to hear the FBI was standing down so that they could send another US Marshal instead, but witness protection was governed by the Marshals Service. So maybe the Marshals were feeling territorial about her.

"You'll have to wait in the interrogation room," Felicia said, gesturing toward it. She yawned widely. "Unfortunately, I need to head home for some sleep before I crash and burn."

"Thanks again, for everything," Mia said sincerely. "Truly, you've been wonderful to believe us when so many others didn't."

"Not a problem." Felicia's smile faded. "I guess you'll be gone by the time I show up for work tonight."

"Yeah." Acting on impulse, Mia hugged the female cop. "I'll miss you. Take care of yourself."

"You too." Felicia hugged her back, then turned away. "Be safe, Mia."

Mia sank into the chair and stared at the four walls surrounding her. She had no idea how long it would take for the new marshal to arrive, and she reminded herself that patience was a virtue.

But she soon found that sitting and waiting all alone was worse than she could have imagined. In the short time she and Cooper had been together, she'd grown accustomed to his presence beside her. Not that he was a chatty man by any stretch of the imagination, but she still missed him.

Deep down, she knew her heart would always belong to Cooper Orchard.

"COOPER? ARE YOU LISTENING TO ME?" Hailey's tone was light and teasing. "Or are you still fixated on your girlfriend?"

He pulled himself together with an effort, eyeing Hailey and Rock who were seated across from him. Hailey and Rock had insisted on taking him out to lunch, and he'd agreed, even though he knew he should be working.

One sketch, even with a nice tip, didn't come close to making up for the days he'd lost.

Yet it wasn't every day a guy met up with his long-lost sister. "She's not my girlfriend."

"Yeah, so you keep saying." Hailey smirked, but then frowned. "What is going on anyway? What danger is she in?"

He tried to come up with an answer that was vague yet satisfying enough that Hailey and Rock would drop it. Although learning Rock was a Park Ranger made him realize his law enforcement instincts would make it difficult to let this go.

"Mia's story isn't mine to tell," he said solemnly. "Suffice it to say, she's only in danger because she did the right thing in coming forward to report a crime. And it doesn't matter now, she's safe at the Gatlinburg police station. I'm sure the FBI has already come to pick her up."

"The FBI?" Hailey echoed. "That sounds big time."

"She must be a federal witness," Rock added. "Let me guess, WITSEC?"

Cooper sighed. "As I said, it's her story to tell and the less you both know, the better. Bad enough she nearly lost her life." He truly didn't want to talk about Mia. It was painful enough to know she was already out of reach.

Forever.

His chest tightened to the point he couldn't breathe. Dear Lord, what had he done?

"I know Sergeant Kellen," Rock said. "He's a decent cop and a good guy."

Cooper nodded. "Yeah, he seems to be on top of things."

"Cooper, look at me." Hailey leaned forward, her gaze drilling into his. "If you care about Mia, then you should go and be with her."

"It's not that easy." He forced himself to scan the menu, although he wasn't very hungry. Then he set it aside. "Tell me about Sawyer and Darby. What are they doing?"

"You're changing the subject," Hailey said with a sigh. "Sawyer is a cop in Chattanooga, and Darby lives in Knoxville with her fiancé and their son, Leo."

"Sawyer's a cop? Darby has a son? Wow." He shook his head and grinned. "That sounds wonderful for both of them." And made him feel like a bit of a failure.

"Sawyer is engaged too," Hailey confided. She glanced at Rock. "We're getting married mid-October in the church across the street from where you were sketching today. We would love to have you join us."

"I'd be honored." He was honestly happy for the both of

them, they looked great together. He found it curious that Hailey and Rock were getting married in a church but didn't ask.

"You really haven't heard from Trent lately?" Hailey asked. "Sawyer mentioned how the two of you took off on your own, years ago."

"We did, yes." He flushed, then said honestly, "Sawyer was bossy, kept telling us what to do. Trent really didn't like it, and I decided to stick with him. I guess it makes sense now that I know Sawyer became a cop."

"Yeah, and a good one," Hailey said defensively. "He broke up a sex-trafficking ring in Chattanooga and saved his fiancé Naomi's life. But I know he was worried about you, Cooper. He'll be thrilled to know you're alive and well. Unfortunately, I'm bummed we don't know where Trent is."

"I'm sure Trent is fine. He plays guitar for the Jimmy Woodrow Band, so that's probably keeping him busy." At least, he hoped so. Cooper took a long drink of his water. "Hard to believe that Jayme and Caitlyn are the only fosters that we haven't seen or heard from."

"I know. Sawyer has been trying to find them, but no luck so far." Hailey's expression was troubled. "Do you know what Trent is using for a last name? That may help us find him."

"Trent Atkins. Apparently, he remembered his real last name, unlike me." The early years of his life were nothing but a blur. It was only his time with the Preacher that he remembered with stark clarity. Despite how much he'd rather forget. He managed a grim smile. "I made mine up, but we both have driver's licenses and IDs."

"Trent Atkins," Hailey repeated. "That's a place to

start. And don't feel bad, my ID is fake too." He had to smile at how Rock grimaced at that. "Sawyer will be very glad to have Trent's information. We've been hoping the others are alive and well."

"Yeah." He understood what Hailey meant. In some ways it was a miracle they'd survived at all. Living on the streets hadn't been easy, worse so, he guessed, for the girls. He and Trent had dodged their share of predators, using teamwork to get away relatively unscathed. He could only imagine what Hailey, Darby, Jayme, and Caitlyn had faced.

It shamed him to realize that he hadn't tried to find any of them. Sure, he'd thought about them at times, but that was it. Apparently, his selfishness knew no bounds. Looking out for himself was understandable in the beginning, but now that he was twenty-six years old, it made him feel petty.

"I should have done more." The words popped out of his mouth before he could call them back.

"Cooper, don't." Hailey reached across the table to touch his arm. "I know you're thinking about what may have happened to the others, but there's no sense in thinking the worst. We survived, there's every reason to believe they did as well."

"Yeah." He forced a smile. "I'll try to remember that."

"Now, about Mia." Hailey sat back in her seat. "You must have a way to contact her, right?"

"No." And suddenly the thought of never seeing her again filled him with panic. "Listen, I need to go."

"Go where?" Hailey demanded. "Can't you finish your lunch first?"

"No. I'll try to find you later, or you can find me. I'm usually working the sidewalk in tourist season." He jumped to his feet, grabbed his knapsack, and quickly threaded his way through the tables.

A sense of urgency hit him hard. What if he was too late? Why had he waited so long? What if she was already gone? He knew it was highly likely she'd already been taken someplace safe by the FBI.

Would Kellen or Zurich know more? Was he crazy to try and find Mia? And to what end? There was no way for this to work out between them. Mia absolutely needed to be safe from Junior.

Unless . . . he gulped and dodged a group of tourists. Was he really going to give up his life, his foster family to go into WITSEC?

Everything inside him recoiled from that thought, but at the same time, he knew Mia was an important part of his life.

Maybe even the most important part.

Sitting across from Hailey, watching the casual intimacy between her and Rock, had touched a nerve. It was exactly the sort of relationship he'd had with Mia. Simply being with her had been like a balm to his soul.

Her kisses were intense and overwhelming, like nothing he'd ever experienced before, which sounded crazy since he and Trent had once prided themselves on dating one woman right after the other.

And most importantly, Mia's faith and relationship with God, something he'd found oddly comforting yet elusive.

He sincerely cared about his foster siblings. Hailey, Sawyer, Trent, Darby, Jayme, and Caitlyn—seeing them again was something he'd never allowed himself to even consider, much less dream about. Especially Trent. He missed his brother, more than he could say.

But Mia . . . his chest ached so much he almost doubled over in pain. He called himself all kinds of a fool as he lightly jogged on his already sore feet, his backpack digging into his shoulders as he took one street, then the next. He searched for every back road that would keep him away from prying eyes while reaching the police station as quickly as possible.

When he caught a glimpse of a police car through the trees, he stopped, instinctively seeking cover. It was a Gatlinburg police cruiser, but it was just sitting there, doing nothing. The car engine wasn't running, which he thought was strange. How could the cop behind the wheel give chase upon catching someone speeding or breaking some other law?

He rested against a tree trunk, unable to take his gaze from the squad. It wasn't as if a cop would have parked it there to walk to a nearby restaurant for lunch.

No, something about the police car was off. And he thought about the Gatlinburg police car that he'd seen driving through Pigeon Forge.

The same one? If so, why?

Cooper didn't want to believe he was imagining things. He decided to get a bit closer, to see if someone was behind the wheel. If the squad was empty because the officer had gone off to check something, then fine. He'd move on his merry way.

The knapsack was unwieldy, but he couldn't make himself leave it behind. Staying low, he drew from his former skills of evasion to ease silently from one tree to the next. He made sure not to draw any attention to himself, and the good thing about his pack was that it was olive green, blending nicely into the forest.

There. He sank to his knees, peering at the squad.

There was absolutely someone sitting behind the wheel. Doing what? He had no clue.

It occurred to Cooper that the cop could be simply on break, maybe catching a quick nap. Not all cops were like Sawyer, who he knew with absolute certainty would never sleep on the job.

Then the figure behind the wheel moved. Okay, so not asleep.

Waiting for someone? The dark head behind the wheel moved from one side to the other. Yeah, it seemed like the only explanation.

Cooper wanted to get close enough to get a look at the cop. If he could see the guy's profile, he felt certain he'd be able to match the image with the man he'd seen in Pigeon Forge.

And if they were one and the same, he'd call Officer Zurich. Or Sergeant Kellen.

He reluctantly eased the pack off his back. Getting closer was a risk, he didn't need his knapsack to trip him up. But he took a moment to dig out his phone. It was only charged to 15%. Great.

After assessing his surroundings, Cooper decided on the best path forward. He needed to be parallel to the passenger side window. The driver's side was facing the road, so getting close there wasn't an option.

Leaving his pack behind the tree, Cooper slithered through the brush on his belly, moving with excruciating slowness. This part of being on the run he hadn't missed, although he hadn't forgotten how to stay hidden. He thought about how much Mia had hated the time they'd spent in the woods. The memory of how upset she'd been at eating a bug made him smile.

When he judged he was close enough, he edged up

onto his knees, peering through the bushes. The person behind the wheel was facing his driver's side window, making it impossible for Cooper to see his profile.

The scrub of facial hair along the guy's jaw indicated the cop was a man.

Come on, come on, he silently urged. *Face the front. Or better yet, turn to look this way, toward me.*

He waited for what seemed like forever before the guy swung his gaze around in his direction. Cooper froze, his heart lodging in his throat when he saw the man's face.

Same guy who was driving through Pigeon Forge. He was certain of it.

But he didn't dare move, not even to slap a mosquito buzzing in his face. The cop appeared to be alert, clearly looking for something.

Or someone.

Mia? Ice congealed in his blood.

After another twenty agonizing seconds, the guy turned to look out the windshield. Cooper didn't hesitate to ease back down so that he was once again lying on his stomach. Despite having his phone, he inched backward through the brush until he was out of the cop's line of sight.

If the guy in there really was a cop. Cooper had no way of knowing for sure.

When he reached his backpack, he finally pulled out his phone. He called Felicia Zurich first, but his call went straight to voice mail. Was she finally sleeping? Probably.

He swallowed hard and called 911. Then he hung up before the call could go through. What if the guy in the squad had his radio on? Would he hear the 911 call? Cooper wasn't sure how it worked, but he wasn't about to bank his life on it.

Or Mia's.

Hadn't Sergeant Kellen given him a card? He quickly dug through his knapsack but came up empty-handed.

Okay, he couldn't afford to waste any more time. He'd have to get past this cop and into the police station as quickly as humanly possible.

Oh yeah, and without getting caught.

He turned to retrace his steps. After purposefully using back roads, he now decided he was better going on the main highway.

And why hadn't he taken Hailey's or Rock's phone numbers? Because he was an idiot, that's why.

When Cooper decided he was far enough away from the parked squad, he looped the backpack over his shoulders and picked up his pace. He wanted that cop to stay right where he was until Sergeant Kellen could verify the guy was legit.

Ten minutes later, he was at the police station. He quickly went inside. "I need to talk to Sergeant Kellen right away."

The woman behind the desk didn't bat an eye. "He's busy."

"This is important." Cooper took a step toward her. "Please, I know he's probably meeting with the FBI about Mia, but there's a cop parked along the side of the building that I saw earlier today in Pigeon Forge. Please, call him. I promise this won't take long."

The woman sighed and picked up her phone. Cooper could only hear her side of the conversation, brief as it was.

"Yes, sir, I'll send him through." The woman replaced the receiver and held out her hand. "I need to search your knapsack."

"How about I leave it here?" He didn't want to waste another moment. The cop could already have moved on.

"No, how about you let me search it to make sure you're not carrying a bomb?" She wiggled her fingers. "Now, please."

He handed her the knapsack, tapping his foot impatiently as she methodically searched it. Without a word, she handed it back. "You should be glad Sergeant Kellen is willing to see you. He's waiting in Interview A."

The same room he and Mia had been in earlier. The room where the walls had begun to close in on him, giving him the same feeling of claustrophobia that he'd experienced while being locked in the Preacher's cellar.

There was no time to worry about that now. "Thanks." He went through the door and quickly found the room. He was shocked to see Mia was still there, but he didn't bother to ask about the delay. "Sergeant Kellen? There's an officer sitting in a squad along the east side of the building. The car is not running, and the driver is the same man I saw driving the Gatlinburg police car in Pigeon Forge."

The news made Kellen frown. "I heard about that from Zurich. Did you get a plate number?"

"No." Cooper bit back a wave of frustration. "But I can show you where he is."

"Okay, let's go." Kellen rose and strode to the door.

"Wait!" Mia jumped up. "I'm coming with you."

"No, you're not," Cooper said sharply. "You need to stay here where it's safe."

"I'm coming," she insisted. "Stop arguing and let's go."

Kellen muttered something beneath his breath, and Cooper knew the guy wasn't happy. "Can't you make her stay here?" Cooper demanded.

"How? By handcuffing her to the table?" Kellen waved a hand. "She's not under arrest, so no. Come on, let's go."

Cooper was surprised and somewhat confused when

Kellen headed out the back. "Do you plan to drive? Or go on foot?"

"On foot." Kellen glanced at him over his shoulder. "You said he's sitting to the east of here, right?"

"Yes." Cooper agreed.

"It's not that far. You can point me in the right direction."

"Okay." Cooper had a bad feeling about this. He hoped the sergeant wasn't going to just walk up to the car and demand the guy roll down his window.

But Cooper hadn't given the seasoned cop enough credit. After threading through several squads, the sergeant hunkered down and pulled a pair of binoculars off his belt. For several long moments, he scanned the area.

"Southeast," Cooper whispered. "There's a road lined with trees and brush on one side."

Another pause. "Yeah, okay. I see it." Kellen peered through the binoculars for a long moment before he lowered the binoculars. His expression appeared to have been carved from stone. "I don't recognize him. He's not Officer Huber, that's for sure."

Cooper assumed Huber was the officer who should have been behind the wheel. "Do you know where Huber is?"

"No. Although someone should have alerted me if Huber didn't check in as usual." Kellen scowled, his expression grim. "Cooper, you get Mia back inside the police station. I need other officers to assist me in taking this guy down."

A loud crack had Cooper yanking Mia down behind the squad. "Gunfire," he croaked.

But Kellen was already speaking into his radio, using

numerical codes that Cooper didn't understand, ending with, "Shots fired, repeat, shots fired."

Cooper curled his body over Mia's, determined to protect her.

And for the second time in his life, he prayed.

CHAPTER FOURTEEN

Mia hadn't been able to see the man in the squad before Cooper dragged her down, covering her with his body. She could hear his heart pounding, or maybe it was hers.

When she'd first seen Cooper coming into the interview room, she'd hoped he'd come back for her. Instead, he'd alerted the sergeant about a squad parked nearby.

Possibly a fake cop. There had already been an attempt to impersonate a US Marshal, why not a cop?

It was all so mind-boggling. This kind of thing only happened in books or movies. Not in real life.

Not to her.

Except it had. She'd watched Frank Germaine kill her father and stepmother in cold blood without displaying an ounce of remorse.

And she had no doubt Frankie would do the same once he found her.

A bevy of uniformed officers swarmed the area, spreading out around them. She couldn't see what was going on because of the way Cooper had her plastered against him, but that was okay.

She was secretly glad for the opportunity to be with him one last time. Although she could have done without the bullets flying around. Mia sent up a quick prayer asking for God's blessing over all of them as they tracked this guy down and arrested him.

There were no additional sounds of gunfire, just the shouts and running footsteps of officers as they took their positions. Mia tried to straighten, but Cooper didn't budge.

"Stay down," he said in a low voice. "I don't want you to be hurt."

"I don't want you hurt either." She breathed in his unique scent, trying to imprint it on her memory.

Another gunshot echoed sharply around them, and she instinctively burrowed closer to Cooper. But then she heard a series of shouts.

"Drop your weapon! Place your hands on your head and get out of the car! Now!"

There was nothing but silence for several long moments, but then she heard, "Suspect is in custody."

"Officer Huber?" Kellen asked.

"No, sir, but he has Huber's badge and gun." There was another silence before the rest of the information came out. "There's a dead body in the trunk of the squad. Appears to be Officer Huber."

Mia sucked in a harsh breath. "He killed a cop? Was that how he knew so much about where we were?"

"Possibly. Get the suspect inside and clear the area," Kellen ordered. "Get the ME out here, stat. I also have two civilian witnesses here that need to be secured."

There was a chorus of ten-fours as the officers began the job securing the area. Mia grappled with the fact that Frankie's men had killed a cop. First a US Marshal, then a local cop.

How many more would die at Frankie's hands before he found her?

Logically, she knew this wasn't her fault. But a heavy shaft of guilt hit hard. Killing all these people, killing her, wouldn't bring Frank Senior back.

But it seemed Frankie didn't care as long as his warped view of justice had been served.

After what seemed like eons, Cooper straightened and helped her upright. Cooper stayed close to her side as additional officers crowded around them.

"I'd like you to let me know if you recognize the suspect," Kellen said, eyeing both of them. He pinned Cooper with a look. "You said you recognized the guy's profile as the cop cruising through Pigeon Forge, correct?"

"Yes." Cooper gave a curt nod. "Happy to take another look to make sure he's the same guy."

"Okay, and you"—Kellen gestured at Mia—"I'd like to know if you recognize him from your dealings with the Germaine family."

"I'll do my best, but I only know Frank Senior by sight. I might recognize Frankie as he supposedly looks like his father."

"All I can ask is that you try." The sergeant's expression was grim, and she knew he was thinking about his murdered officer. "Don't worry, we'll make sure he can't see either of you."

Two officers flanked her and Cooper as they headed back inside the police station. By the shocked expressions on their faces, Mia suspected this kind of thing didn't happen often. Gatlinburg wasn't a high crime metropolis like Chicago had been.

And it was her fault that all of this was taking place in the normally quiet tourist town.

Well, more accurately, Frankie Germaine's fault.

The officers ushered them back into the interview room. Because her knees were a little shaky, she dropped into the closest chair. Cooper sat next to her, and she put a hand on his arm.

"You were amazing," she said in a hushed tone. "I can't even imagine what might have happened if you hadn't seen that guy sitting in the stolen police car."

"Thanks, but it feels like too little, too late," Cooper admitted. "It's awful to think that the dead cop was in the trunk the entire time."

"I know." She closed her eyes for a moment. "We need to say a prayer for him. Officer Huber died in the line of duty."

"Agree." He covered her hand with his.

"Lord, bless Officer Huber and bring him home to You. Amen."

"Amen," Cooper said. He cleared his throat, then asked, "Why are you still here anyway? I thought the FBI was coming to pick you up? They should have been here by now."

Mia took heart that Cooper had participated in her brief prayer and smiled wearily. "Turns out once the FBI contacted the US Marshals Service, they decided to send a Marshal instead."

Cooper rolled his eyes. "Politics? Really?"

She shrugged. "More like who has jurisdiction, which honestly belongs to the Marshals. Especially since one of their own was murdered." She swallowed hard. "Just like Officer Huber."

"Those deaths are not your fault, Mia."

"I know, but still." She blew out a breath. "When will it end?"

He slowly shook his head. "Probably not until Junior is in custody."

"Yeah." She forced a smile. "Tell me about your reunion with Hailey."

"It's incredible to think she's been here about as long as I have, yet our paths didn't cross until today. She lives and works away from the downtown area, which is where I've spent all my time. Hailey and Rock seem really happy together."

"Did you learn about your other foster siblings?" Mia had tried not to be upset that he hadn't told her more about the kids he'd lived with. He'd told her about the abuse and the fire but hadn't gone into detail about the rest, other than telling her their names.

"Yeah. Sawyer is a cop in Chattanooga, and Darby lives in Knoxville with her fiancé and son, Leo." He looked bemused. "It seems surreal. I guess I honestly never expected we'd ever find each other, not after all this time."

"Had you searched for them?"

His expression clouded. "No. The only person I stayed in touch with was Trent. And I never heard back after my recent call."

"I'm sorry, I didn't mean to insinuate you should have been searching for them." She mentally kicked herself for making him sad. "It's understandable that you would focus on moving forward, not looking backward."

"I was selfish," Cooper said bluntly. "I was focused on myself rather than opening myself up to others." He lifted his head and met her gaze straight on. "Until you, Mia. These past few days have been eye-opening for me, to say the least."

She tried to read his expression. "Eye-opening in a good way? Or a not so good way?"

"Mostly good." His grin was lopsided. "It's never easy to take a hard look at yourself, acknowledging your flaws."

"But we all have flaws, Cooper. That's why God sent Jesus to walk among us. *For God so loved the world that He gave his one and only Son, that whoever believes in him shall not perish but have eternal life.* John 3:16."

"I'm not sure I'm worthy of that," Cooper admitted.

"None of us are worthy," she gently corrected him. "But God forgives us anyway."

He mulled that over. "You may be right about that. Each time I prayed, I experienced a sense of peace."

Her heart lifted in joy. "Oh, Cooper. That happens to me too. God will gladly shoulder our burdens, all we have to do is follow His path and His will."

"Sounds easier said than done." His tone was wry.

"Maybe but look at how far you've come. How far God has brought you." She leaned over to press a kiss to his cheek. "God has never given up on you, Cooper. Not even in your darkest days. And I believe that fire was God's way of helping you and the other foster kids escape."

"I'd never considered that possibility," he admitted.

Before she could say anything more, there was a brief knock at the door. It opened and Sergeant Kellen poked his head in. "Do either of you need anything? We're still processing the perp and the crime scene, but it shouldn't be much longer."

"Lunch would be nice," Mia said. "If it's not a problem."

"Yeah, I could eat," Cooper added.

"I'll send out for sandwiches." The sergeant glanced at his watch. "We hope to have you make the ID very soon. Sit tight."

"Okay, thanks." Mia sat back in her chair. "Once we've finished with this, you'll be able to get back to sketching."

Cooper didn't say anything for a long moment. Then he turned his chair to face her. "Mia, I came back because of you. It was sheer luck that I stumbled across the guy sitting in the squad."

"Not luck," she countered. "God was guiding you to him, Cooper. You helped bring another bad guy to justice." Then the impact of his words sank deep. "I don't understand. Why did you want to see me again?"

"I don't want to lose you." His expression was serious, and she could tell he'd agonized over this decision. "I would like to ask the US Marshals to relocate us, together."

Her heart swelled with hope, but she tamped it down with an effort. "Cooper, as much as I'd like nothing more than to have you as part of my life, I won't ask you to give up your family. Hailey, Sawyer, Trent, Darby . . ." Her voice trailed off. "You've just found Hailey, haven't even reunited yet with Sawyer and Darby. And I'm sure you'll eventually hear from Trent and find the others." At least she hoped so. "You were right to stay here. This is your life, Cooper." She hesitated, then added, "And you deserve to be happy."

"I can't be happy without you, Mia." He regarded her steadily. "I just about had a panic attack over the possibility of never ever seeing you again. Of not even having a way to contact you."

"Oh, Cooper." Tears welled in her eyes. "I feel the same way about not being able to see you. But I also don't want you to regret giving up your family." She sighed, then added, "Once you make this decision, there's no going back. I'm worried you'll grow to resent me if you do this without thinking it through."

The door opened again, revealing Sergeant Kellen. "Okay, are you ready to do this?"

Mia nodded and stood. Cooper did the same.

"He's located on the other side of the building," Kellen explained as he led the way through the cubicles and desks. "You'll be seeing him through one-way glass. He won't be able to see you."

Mia instinctively reached out to take Cooper's hand. "Got it."

Sergeant Kellen stopped and gestured to a window. "Take a look, see if you recognize him from anywhere."

It took more courage than she wanted to admit to step forward and peer through the glass. The minute she saw the man's face she gasped.

"What? You know him?" Kellen asked sharply.

She blinked and looked again to make sure she wasn't mistaken. "Yes," she said in a low voice. "He's a Chicago cop, or at least he was."

Cooper tightened his grip on her hand. "He's the same guy I saw driving through Pigeon Forge," he added.

Kellen frowned, his gaze locked on hers. "Explain what you mean."

She drew in a deep breath. "I told you how I witnessed Frank Germaine shooting my father and my stepmother. I managed to escape, mostly because Frank didn't know I was there. But when I was out on the street, I saw this police car parked two blocks from my dad's house. I went over and that man"—she gestured to the guy in the room—"was behind the wheel. At first he brushed me off, saying he was in the middle of something, but when I said my name, he tried to get me into the car. I didn't like his abrupt change in attitude, so I ran. He followed in his cruiser, but I managed to jump in a taxi and escape."

"Well, well, isn't that interesting." Kellen nodded thoughtfully. "A dirty cop, likely on Frank Germaine's payroll. That might explain how those two idiots kept finding you. We think he may have had Huber's squad for a while now. Let's see how loyal he is to his current employer now that we can pin a murder on him."

Mia swallowed hard. "It's good I recognized him, but I was really hoping the guy was Frankie."

"I'm sure the Feds will find him," Sergeant Kellen said reassuringly. "Especially if we can convince Louis here to talk."

"Louis what?" Cooper asked.

"Louis Strawn." Kellen arched a brow. "Is the name familiar?"

"No, sorry," Cooper said.

"Not to me either." Mia shivered. "I'm just glad I didn't get into his car."

"Okay, well, you've both been very helpful," Sergeant Kellen said. "Mia, I expect the US Marshals will be here by the time you finish eating. I had the sandwiches placed in the interview room for you."

"Thanks." Mia turned away from Louis Strawn. As much as she was glad the dirty cop had been apprehended, she'd really hoped to find that Frankie was the one in custody. But it was clear Frankie Germaine was still out there, somewhere.

No matter what Cooper said a few minutes ago, she couldn't let him come with her.

Frankie was the one who wanted her dead. With the two guys and the dirty cop arrested, she was confident Cooper would be safe here in Gatlinburg.

With his family, where he belonged.

COOPER FOLLOWED Mia back to the interview room. Their sandwiches and bottles of water were waiting on the table for them.

Mia said a quick prayer, then looked at him. "You should take your sandwich to go." Mia took a sip of her water, then unwrapped her sandwich. "You'll be safe now that Louis and the others have been arrested. Frankie doesn't likely know much about you."

"I'm staying." Leaving Gatlinburg wasn't an easy choice to make, yet he knew it was the right one. At least Hailey knew he was fine, and she'd be sure to tell the other foster kids that too. He regretted not being able to talk to Trent one last time, but there wasn't anything he could do about that now.

Besides, Trent hadn't returned his call. So that pretty much told him his foster brother had moved on to bigger and better things.

"Cooper, please." Mia's gaze clung to his. "I know how important your art and your family are to you. Don't make this decision based on hormones."

"Hormones?" He almost burst out laughing. "Trust me, I'm not." He leaned closer. "I think I've fallen in love with you, Mia. I know we haven't been together for long, so it's hard to say for sure, but I can't imagine my life without you."

"Oh, Cooper." Her large dark eyes glinted with tears. "I love you too. But I know your art and your siblings are just as important."

"They are, but so are you." He wanted to pull her into his arms but forced himself to eat the meal before him.

Mia looked upset, and he couldn't help feeling a bit wounded. He'd thought she'd be thrilled to have him go with her. How could she claim she loved him while looking so miserable?

Neither of them spoke for long minutes. "We're in this together, Mia, remember?" He searched her gaze. "And who knows, maybe someday, once they arrest Junior, we'll be safe enough so that we can return to Gatlinburg." Then he realized she may not want to live in such a small, tourist town and forced himself to add, "Or Chicago, if that's what you'd prefer."

"Gatlinburg is warmer than Chicago." Her smile didn't reach her eyes. "But I still think you should stay here. If Frankie is arrested, then I can always come back."

"*When* Junior is arrested," he said firmly. "You were the one who said we need to think positive, right?"

"Yes." After swallowing another bite of her sandwich, she added, "Which is why I think you should stay here in Gatlinburg for a while. You heard what Sergeant Kellen said about how Louis will likely give them the information they need to find Frankie." This time, her smile seemed genuine. "It's only a matter of time."

"And if he doesn't?" Cooper shook his head. "I've already chosen you, Mia. When they arrest Frankie, we'll reunite with my foster siblings. But until then, we stick together no matter what."

She eyed him over the rim of her water bottle. "You seem pretty sure about this."

"I am." Deep down, he knew this was the right decision. Mia was his hope, his future. And maybe he couldn't sketch tourists for a living, but there was nothing to stop him from sketching in private.

"Excuse me a moment." Mia pushed her half-eaten sandwich aside and stood. "Just need to use the restroom."

"Sure." He continued eating, wondering where he and

Mia would end up. Did they get any input as to where they'd be relocated? He'd never seen the ocean and wouldn't mind being somewhere near water. If not the ocean, maybe a lake or even a river.

He tried not to panic at the thought of what he'd do for a job. Nothing involving drawing, that's for sure. But definitely something that enabled him to be outside. Hailey had mentioned how she worked at Rhodes Hobby Farm. Something like that wouldn't be too bad.

After about five minutes, he frowned. What on earth was taking Mia so long? He opened the door and glanced around.

Sergeant Kellen was talking to another officer, so he had to wait until they'd finished. "Sorry to bother you, but where's Mia? Did you need more information from her?"

Kellen gave him an odd look. "No, she's with the US Marshal who just arrived."

A wave of dread washed over him. "Did you verify the guy is legit?"

"His name is Mark Beldon, and he's legit," Kellen assured him. "I think they just left."

"Left?" A sense of betrayal hit hard. Cooper hastily turned and rushed through the police station until he was outside. "Mia, wait!"

Mia was standing beside a tall man who appeared to be in his midforties, wearing a cowboy hat and a five-point marshal badge on his chest. They were near a dark blue Dodge Ram pickup truck.

Mia reluctantly turned to face him. "Please, Cooper. Let me go. You need to stay here with your family."

"I can't believe you sneaked out without even saying goodbye!" He couldn't hold back his anger and disappointment. "So much for loving me, huh, Mia?"

"Enough." The marshal lifted his hand, warning Cooper to stay where he was. "Son, you need to stay right where you are. This isn't your concern."

Not his concern? The woman he loved more than anything was leaving without so much as saying goodbye.

"Please, Cooper." Tears streamed down Mia's face, slicing through his anger. "I'm begging you to stay with your family."

"Why?" He truly didn't understand why she was doing this.

"Get into the truck, Mia," the US Marshal said as he stepped in front of her.

Crack!

For the second time in a number of hours, the sound of gunfire echoed around them. The US Marshal staggered and fell against Mia, pinning her against the side of the truck as a red stain bloomed on his upper chest.

He'd been shot!

CHAPTER FIFTEEN

A flash from the wooded area to the east of the police station caught his eye. Cops swarmed from the building, including Sergeant Kellen. Cooper took off toward the woods, hoping at least a few of the officers would follow him.

He wasn't going to let this guy get away.

Maybe if they were able to get enough of these men to turn against Junior, they'd be able to find and arrest him.

When he reached the trees, he ducked down and listened. He knew it wouldn't take long for the Gatlinburg police to head this way.

In fact, that was exactly what he was hoping for.

Cooper wasn't a cop, but he did know how to hunt in the woods.

He waited and watched, hoping the shooter hadn't already disappeared.

The cops were coming closer, but he didn't move, didn't take his eyes off his surroundings. He'd seen the flash of movement and hoped he'd see it again.

Show me the way, Lord.

The prayer echoed unbidden through his mind. Then he saw another movement coming from his right, just a few yards from where he was.

Got you, he thought with grim satisfaction.

He abruptly sprang to his feet, lunging toward the spot, mentally braced for the impact of a bullet. He hadn't really considered the danger he was facing. His only goal was to bring this guy down.

Before he killed Mia.

Cooper must have caught the shooter off guard because he staggered backward, belatedly bringing up his gun. Cooper ignored the weapon, barreling into the man with all the strength he could muster.

Cooper's momentum sent them both to the ground, the impact snapping the shooter's head against the ground. Not hard enough to knock him unconscious, but long enough for Cooper to lean hard against his neck.

Where was the gun? Cooper didn't know, but if the guy still had it, he felt certain he'd have already been shot.

The man began to struggle against him. Cooper tightened his grip, using everything he had to hang on, despite the fact that the shooter was bigger and more muscular than he was.

"Cooper!" Sergeant Kellen's shout was reassuring, but Cooper didn't let up. He needed to cut off this guy's air supply long enough for the police to get him into custody.

"Cooper!" The shout was closer, followed by the pounding of footsteps against the earth, but Cooper didn't take his gaze off the gunman.

The guy continued to fight, punching Cooper in the back and shoulders, but he was growing weaker due to the lack of oxygen. Cooper didn't let up until the shooter fell limp, and the cops had joined him.

"Thanks, but we'll take him from here," Kellen said gruffly. "Are you okay?"

Cooper rolled off the gunman, the reality of what had just happened hitting hard. He stared upright at the streaks of sunlight through the trees. Then he abruptly sat up and looked around.

"How's Mia? And the marshal?" Cooper staggered to his feet. Adrenaline raced through his bloodstream, making him feel shaky.

"We're getting the marshal the medical attention he needs, the bullet hit the upper part of his chest. I need you to stay right where you are, Cooper." Kellen raked his gaze over the ground until he found the gun. "Well, well, what do we have here." Kellen's tone was laced with grim satisfaction. The sergeant gestured to one of his officers. "I want this weapon bagged for evidence, and we'll need to check this guy's hands for gunpowder residue as well before we take his fingerprints to match them to whatever we can find on the gun. I want this scene processed by the book, understand?"

"Got it," the cop nearest to Kellen said.

"I need to see Mia." Cooper was glad to have helped bring down the shooter, but he was still upset by the way Mia had planned to leave without him. "Please, Sergeant. I have to see her."

"Okay, give me a minute." Kellen watched as two cops cuffed the shooter, who was beginning to show signs of waking up. The sergeant knelt beside him. "Who are you?"

"Lawyer," the man croaked.

"Yeah, sure. You'll get your lawyer. You'll need a good one since you've shot a federal officer. That means being placed in a federal prison, with bad guys far worse than you." Kellen smiled without humor.

There was a hint of fear in the shooter's eyes before he glanced away.

The two officers who'd cuffed him dragged him to his feet and began to pat him down, searching for more weapons before escorting him to the police station. *The Gatlinburg jail cells must be full by now*, Cooper thought wearily, there had never been a crime spree like this one as far back as he could remember.

And every single suspect was likely hired by Junior.

"Hey, what's this?" One of the cops held up a five-point badge. "Looks like this guy is the fake marshal."

Cooper turned to stare at the handcuffed perp. Kellen narrowed his eyes as the other officer pulled marshal credentials out of his pocket. "Oh, the Feds are going to love taking you into custody." Kellen gestured to the officers. "Bag all of that as evidence too."

"Will do, Sarge."

Cooper turned and hurried back toward the parking lot outside the police station. He'd been so focused on taking down the gunman he hadn't heard the sirens, but two ambulances sat in the parking lot, red lights spinning as paramedics gathered around the injured marshal.

"Cooper!" Mia's cry came from the doorway of the police station. She broke away from the two officers who flanked her and ran toward him. When she threw herself into his arms, he gladly clutched her close, burying his face in her hair.

This was where she belonged, whether she realized it or not.

"You're not hurt?" he managed to ask.

"Me? You're the one who took off after a man with a

gun." She lifted her face from his chest, her arms locked around his waist. "What were you thinking? He could have shot you!"

"I wasn't going to let him get away." He gazed for a long moment into her big beautiful brown eyes. "I love you, Mia. I'm coming with you wherever the Marshals plan to relocate you."

"Oh, Cooper." She shook her head. "I don't know what to do with you."

He wanted to kiss her, but she frowned as the officers brought the gunman toward the building.

She sucked in a harsh breath. "I—I think that's Frankie! I mean, he has a beard, and long hair, but the shape of his face and his eyes are mirror images of his father."

"What?" Cooper loosened his grip so that he could turn to face the gunman. Then he glanced back at Mia. "Are you sure?"

"I think so." Her gaze never wavered from the gunman. "The eyes, the jaw, and his cheekbones are similar. Regardless, I'm pretty sure the Feds will confirm his identity, right, Frankie?" She'd raised her voice so he could hear.

The gunman's face grew red with fury. He spat out a slew of curses, ending with, "You killed my father!"

Cooper instinctively stepped in front of Mia. "Your father is the murderer, and so are you. We'll both make sure you never see the light of day other than through the bars of a prison cell."

That only made Junior erupt into more curses. The two officers dragged him inside the police station.

"I wonder who will turn against him first," Mia said thoughtfully.

"Yeah, good question." He turned and pulled her gently

into his arms. Since talking hadn't seemed to work, he lowered his head and kissed her.

———————

MIA MELTED AGAINST COOPER, her head spinning from the heat of his kiss. Being in his arms felt right, and she realized her attempt to do what was best for him had failed big-time.

After several long minutes, Cooper lifted his head. "I love you, Mia."

Tears misted her eyes. "And I love you too."

"Sorry to break up the romantic moment," a cop drawled, "but Sarge wants you inside."

"Wait, what about Marshal Beldon?" Mia glanced over to where the paramedics were lifting the marshal and placing him on a gurney. "Is he okay? Is he going to survive?"

"All I can tell you is that they're taking him to the University of Tennessee Regional Medical Center. It's the closest trauma center."

"I can't bear the thought of Frankie killing another marshal," she murmured, more to herself than to anyone else. First Sean, now Mark. Yes, she knew both men chose this career, knowing they'd be in danger, but to lose their life because of her?

Not her, she quickly amended. Because of Frankie and his insatiable thirst for revenge.

She forced herself to step away from Cooper, although he quickly took her hand. "Okay, but I'm getting a little tired of Interview A."

Cooper let out a strangled laugh. "Yeah, me too."

Sergeant Kellen was on his cell phone when they

approached. "Yes, we have a strong reason to believe our perp is Frank Germaine Junior. We need you here ASAP."

After a few minutes, Kellen slid his phone into his pocket. "That was the FBI Special Agent in Charge in Knoxville. They're on their way."

"For sure this time?" Mia asked wryly.

Sergeant Kellen nodded. "Beldon getting shot changes things. They want details."

"I saw it happen," Cooper admitted.

"I'm afraid I didn't see much of anything," Mia added. "But of course we'll be happy to talk to them."

"We're still processing our suspect, but we're hoping to get his fingerprints into the system, see what pops." Kellen's expression held anticipation. "I'm hoping he has priors and maybe an outstanding warrant."

"I'm not sure about that." Mia frowned. "Sean told me that Frankie was clean until his father was arrested, which is when he decided to take over the business."

Kellen's expression held disappointment. "We still have him on shooting a federal marshal. That should be enough to hold him without bail. Especially since we found a dead marshal's badge and creds in his possession."

"I wonder if the gun he used belonged to Sean McCarthy too?" Cooper mused. "That would really put him away."

"Oh, he's going away," Kellen said firmly. "Thanks to you, Cooper. Although I should arrest you for interfering with a crime."

Mia straightened. "You wouldn't."

"No, but that doesn't mean I want anything like that to happen again." Kellen drilled Cooper with a narrow glare. "You are not a police officer, remember? It's not your job to apprehend a perp, understand?"

"Yes, but to be honest, I didn't really take time to think it through." Cooper shrugged. "It was sheer gut instinct."

Mia shivered at how close Cooper had come to losing his life. She wasn't sure what had happened or how Cooper had caught Frankie off guard, but she knew that Frankie could have easily shot Cooper and found a way to escape.

God had surely been looking out for them. Especially for Cooper.

"Have a seat, finish your lunch, and the Feds will be here soon." Kellen gestured toward the interview room.

"Such luxurious accommodations," Cooper muttered as they took their respective seats.

She laughed. "Yeah, not." What was left of her sandwich was a bit stale, but she took a bite anyway, especially as there was no way of knowing when their next meal would be.

"I feel terrible about Marshal Beldon," she said, breaking the silence.

"I know." Cooper offered a wan smile. "I pray he makes it."

"Me too." She took another bite. "I still can't believe you caught Frankie."

Cooper shrugged. "It was probably the first time in my life that I did something unselfish."

"That's not true, Cooper." Her tone was sharper than she intended. "You have done plenty of things for me. Starting with following the men who intended to harm me. And offering to come with me into WITSEC. You don't seem to have an accurate view of yourself. God chose you to come into my life for a reason. And I'm very grateful God sent you to help me through this."

There was a long poignant silence before he spoke. "Watching you walk away a second time gutted me," he said quietly. "I don't think I've ever felt that bad, not even when Trent took off for Nashville."

"I'm sorry." She knew her words were inadequate, so she reached over to take his hand. "I wanted you to have the family you deserve. Your foster siblings and your life as an artist. I couldn't ask you to give all that up, Cooper. I still can't ask you to do that."

"You are my life, Mia." He held her gaze intently. "And while you won't ask, know that I'm not letting you go without me."

Stupid tears welled in her eyes. "Letting you go hurt me, more than you know."

"Oh, I think I have an idea." He leaned over to give her a quick kiss. "It's exactly how I let Trent go. He wanted to follow his dream of playing music for adoring fans. I couldn't hold him back from that, so I encouraged him to go."

"Yes." She used her free hand to swipe at her face, realizing he really did understand. "It's only because we care so much that we put that person's needs above our own."

"Exactly." He tightened his grip on her hand. "We're going to stick together from here on, right? No more heading off by yourself."

She sniffled and smiled through her tears. "I promise."

"Good." Cooper let her go, and they finished eating. To her surprise, there was a knock at the door a few minutes later.

Sergeant Kellen poked his head in. "Feds are here."

She immediately tensed. "That's not possible, Knoxville is an hour away."

"Yeah, well, not by chopper." The sergeant shook his head. "I guess Frank Germaine Junior is a big deal. And they're feeling guilty they pushed you off on Beldon in the first place. Stupid politics."

"You verified Junior's identity?" Cooper asked.

"Yep. His prints were on file from when he was seventeen and busted for smoking pot." A sly grin creased Kellen's features. "You gotta love it when the past comes back to bite them in the rear end."

Mia managed a tight smile. "Okay, we're ready to talk to the FBI."

The sergeant disappeared, and two men wearing suits stepped into the room. She rose on shaky legs. "Hello. I'm Mia Royce, formerly Monique Hastings. I provided eyewitness testimony against Frank Germaine Senior for the murder of my father and stepmother."

"And I'm Cooper Orchard, local artist." Cooper stayed close to Mia's side. "We've been running from Junior's men for the past few days."

"And Cooper helped bring Frankie to justice," Mia added.

The two suits nodded. The taller one introduced himself. "I'm Special Agent in Charge Jason Burke. This is Special Agent Tom Lawson. Please take a seat. I'm sorry for the delay in our getting back to you, but we're here now. I'm afraid we'll need you both to start at the beginning."

Mia swallowed a groan but did as asked. Cooper sat next to her, holding her hand beneath the table.

The recounting of the story took longer than she'd imagined, but when they were finished, Jason Burke nodded in satisfaction. "I think that's more than enough to keep Frank Junior behind bars."

"Does Junior have other men out there coming after Mia?" Cooper asked. "I think it's only fair for her to know how much danger she's still in."

The two Feds exchanged a look. "We don't have the answer to that yet. But the fact that Junior, as you call him, was here and doing his own dirty work makes me think there aren't many others out there searching for you."

"Thinking isn't knowing," Cooper pointed out.

Jason Burke lifted a hand. "I understand your concern, but it's going to take us some time to investigate. What we've heard so far is that an administrative assistant inside the US Marshals office leaked information on Sean McCarthy, which is how they found and killed him. From there, they must have found you. As soon as we have other answers, we'll let you know."

Mia was surprised to find out that someone from inside the US Marshals office had leaked info, although it explained a lot. As did learning that Louis, the Chicago cop, had killed a cop to get inside information about their location as well.

At least it was over.

"What happens in the meantime?" Cooper asked. "We've been stuck inside this room for most of the day."

"We're planning to relocate you both to a safe house in Knoxville," Jason said. "That's one of the reasons we brought the chopper."

The idea of flying back to Knoxville was thrilling and terrifying at the same time. But Mia's biggest concern was for Cooper. She tightened her grip on his hand. "Are you sure about this?"

"Absolutely." He spoke without hesitation.

"Okay, then, we'll be ready to go when you are," Mia agreed.

"Give me some time to talk to the men Kellen has in custody." Jason Burke glanced at his watch. "We'll need about an hour."

"Okay, sounds good." Mia watched as the two federal agents stood. When they were gone, she turned toward Cooper. "Last chance," she said only half joking. "There's still time for you to change your mind."

"It hurts that you don't trust me, Mia." Cooper frowned. "What can I do to convince you that I love you?"

She met his gaze. "I believe you love me, as I love you. God brought us together, Cooper. But there's a part of me that is worried you haven't really gotten over your past."

His expression turned thoughtful. "Okay, that's fair. I believe you are right about God bringing us together, Mia. I have instinctively prayed to Him when I needed His guidance. And I should take a moment to thank Him for bringing you into my life."

"Oh, Cooper. That's the sweetest thing anyone has ever said to me." She smiled through misty eyes.

"I know there's a lot for me to learn," he acknowledged. "But I'm willing to do whatever is necessary. Hearing that Hailey and Rock are actually getting married in the church here in town makes me realize how important it is to put the past to rest."

Hearing about a wedding they likely wouldn't be able to attend made her feel sad. "I'm sorry you'll miss their ceremony."

"Stop apologizing," he said without heat. "What can I do to make you trust me in this?"

"Kiss me," she whispered, leaning against him. "I need you to hold me and kiss me, Cooper."

"Now that is no hardship." He pulled her as close as the chairs would allow and kissed her. Mia's heart swelled with love and happiness.

"I love you so much, Mia." He kissed her again. "And I know we're going to be just fine from here on out."

"I know we will." She nestled against him, feeling content. Relocating to a new place, in a new town, in a new state wouldn't be nearly as stressful with Cooper at her side.

And maybe someday, when Frankie and his accomplices were tried and convicted, they'd return to Gatlinburg, Tennessee.

The place Cooper called home.

EPILOGUE

Three weeks later . . .

Cooper didn't mind the landscaping job the US Marshals had helped him obtain. The small apartment he and Mia shared, after a small and private wedding, wasn't the best place in the world, but he'd been in much worse.

Florida was humid and sunny, much like Tennessee, only much hotter. The ocean was amazing, but he secretly missed the Smoky Mountains.

He could only draw in private, and that wasn't easy to live with either, but since Mia didn't mind sitting for him, he was generally content. More so than he'd ever imagined. And that was all because of Mia.

She was worth everything and more.

Mia worked as a receptionist in a medical clinic. The pay wasn't great, they were barely scraping by, but she really enjoyed helping her elderly patients and had recently asked US Deputy Marshal Eric Sutton to allow her to take nursing courses. She already had the basic science college credits under her belt and wanted to move forward with a nursing career. Deputy Mark

Beldon had survived and was still recuperating from surgery.

Cooper often wondered how Hailey, Rock, Sawyer, Trent, Darby, and the other fosters were doing. He wished he'd been able to spend more than a few minutes with Hailey and Rock, but he was blessed to have had that much. At least Hailey knew he'd survived the Preacher and could tell the others he was doing fine.

Especially Trent. If they'd managed to track him down by now.

Since he was finished for the day, Cooper rode his bicycle to the apartment he shared with Mia. They had one car, courtesy of the US Marshals, but Mia needed it more than he did. He preferred walking or biking to get from one place to another. Old habits died hard.

When he saw a strange vehicle parked on the road, he frowned. The car could have belonged to anyone, but he had the distinct feeling the Feds had dropped by for a visit.

And he was right. When he unlocked the apartment door, he heard Mia say, "Here's Cooper now."

Special Agent in Charge Jason Burke rose to his feet. "Nice to see you again, Cooper."

Cooper couldn't really say he felt the same, but he managed a smile. "What brings you to the Panhandle?"

"Frank Germaine Junior has decided to plead guilty to murdering Deputy Sean McCarthy and the attempted murder of Deputy Mark Beldon in exchange for taking the death penalty off the table." The federal agent looked grim. "We have other charges pending against him too, but those are the ones that will put him away for the rest of his life."

"I'm shocked he agreed to that," Mia said.

"His mistake for killing a man in Tennessee," Burke said with a shrug. "The good news is that his father's empire has fallen apart after we made a series of additional arrests. The two men who you helped the Gatlinburg PD arrest spilled the beans on several others who were also hired by Frankie to find you. They worked in teams, apparently, yet still had trouble keeping you in their sights."

"So they weren't tracking my phone?" Mia asked.

"No."

"Yet they still found us, more than once," Cooper said dryly. He exchanged a look with Mia. "All of this means what exactly?"

Agent Burke spread his hands. "Neither one of you is in danger any longer. If you want to stay in the program, that's fine, but if you want to leave, that's okay too. Your choice either way."

"We'll stay here," Cooper said at the same time Mia said, "We're returning to Gatlinburg."

A smile tugged at the corner of the agent's mouth. "Sounds like you need to talk about it before deciding."

Cooper turned toward Mia. "Our life here isn't bad, Mia. You mentioned going to a nursing program, now you can do that."

"Your family is in Gatlinburg," she argued. "Hailey is important and so are your other foster siblings."

"They are, but that doesn't mean we need to live in the same place. Lots of families visit each other across state lines."

"Please, Cooper. I know your sketching is important to you as is your family. I can look into online nursing programs." She paused, then added, "There's a nursing program in Knoxville, which isn't too far of a commute."

Her willingness to go back to Tennessee with him was humbling. "I want you to be sure, Mia."

"I love you, Cooper." She wrapped her arms around his

neck and kissed him. "And I want to go back home to Tennessee."

It was in that moment he truly understood the power of God's love. And the life he and Mia were blessed to have together.

THANK you for reading *Cooper's Choice*! I hope you loved hearing about how Cooper and Mia's fought danger in order to find happiness. Are you interested in reading Trent and Serena's story in *Trent's Trust*? Click here!

DEAR READER

I hope you enjoyed *Cooper's Choice*, the fourth book in my Smoky Mountain Secrets series. I'm having fun writing about the fosters' reunions and can't wait until they all find each other in *Jayme's Journey*.

Reviews are so important to authors! I would very much appreciate you leaving a review on the platform from which you purchased the book. Thank you so much.

I also adore hearing from my readers! I can be found on Facebook at https://www.facebook.com/LauraScottBooks, Twitter at https://twitter.com/laurascottbooks, Instagram at https://www.instagram.com/laurascottbooks/, and through my website https://www.laurascottbooks.com. If you enjoy my books, you'll want to sign up for my monthly newsletter as I offer a free novella to all subscribers. This novella is not available on any platform, it's exclusive to those of you who join my list.

Thanks again for your support! I'm blessed to have wonderful readers like you!

Until next time,

Laura Scott

P. S. If you're curious about *Trent's Trust*, I've included the first chapter here . . .

TRENT'S TRUST

Trent Atkins put everything he had into his performance yet found it impossible to lose himself in his music. After finishing the song, he sipped his water, glancing surreptitiously at the woman seated near the back of the pub. She was pretty, with straight chin-length blond hair, high cheekbones, and curvy physique, but so far he hadn't seen her smile. The mystery woman had shown up at his last two gigs, but he did not get the groupie vibe from her.

Just the opposite.

She seemed to be sitting there, judging him. Was she someone he'd met when he'd been with the Jimmy Woodrow Band? A one-night stand he'd never contacted again? Or maybe one of Jimmy's one-night stands? He abruptly steered away from thoughts of his buddy's abrupt death or he'd never be able to finish this set.

Trent launched into another song, doing his best to ignore the woman's intense stare. Music had always been his sanctuary. His place of peace. Something he'd lost when he'd joined Jimmy's band. Of course, he hadn't realized it at the time. No, Trent had been drawn toward the lure of raking in big money, being famous, and living large. All of which had come true. At least temporarily. The money had been great, better than anything he'd ever experienced before, but the drinking and drugs soon had the entire band spiraling out of control. He hadn't taken many drugs, but the alcohol? Oh yeah. The booze had been the devil on his shoulder.

But not anymore. At least, not for the past four months. Which he knew wasn't saying much. Trent closed his eyes for a moment and focused on the song. A country rock ballad he'd composed himself after getting and staying sober.

When Trent finished, he tipped his cowboy hat—it was a prop more than anything—to acknowledge the spattering of applause. Then he thanked the crowd for coming and mentioned he'd be playing at the Thirsty Saloon next Friday night too. He stood, looped his guitar crossways over his body, and moved off the small rough plank stage, heading toward the rear door of the bar.

The saloon was a far cry from the high-level clubs the Jimmy Woodrow Band had played in. Jimmy and the band had drawn huge crowds and had more gigs than he'd ever imagined was possible. It had been a roller coaster of a ride.

Until the night Trent woke up, hungover and trying not to puke, only to stumble across Jimmy's dead body on the floor of their hotel suite.

The image haunted him still. Jimmy's wide eyes staring blankly at the ceiling, his body cold to the touch. Since Trent had pretty much passed out, he had no real idea of what had happened.

If he were honest, he didn't want to know. What if he'd somehow played a role in his friend's death? Even after all this time, he was secretly waiting for the police to show up and haul him away in handcuffs.

Especially since Trent had cowardly left the hotel room without waiting around for the authorities to show up. He hadn't even called the police but had huddled in a seedy dive motel room watching TV waiting for the news to explode.

And it certainly had.

Trent was so preoccupied with his thoughts, ruminating over the past, he didn't notice the figure dressed in a black hoodie coming swiftly toward him until it was almost too late. Trent's street-fighting instincts had him lashing out with his foot in an attempt to kick the guy's groin while throwing a punch with his left hand, his dominant one. He also shouted at the top of his lungs, hoping to draw the attention of people passing by.

Out of nowhere, the blonde from the bar showed up and struck the attacker from behind, bringing two fists down onto the back of his head with surprising force. The hooded man stumbled, dropped a knife, then whirled and ran off, darting between the cars in the small parking lot.

Trent gaped at her, trying to understand what had happened. A mugger tried to steal from him, but his mystery woman had charged to his rescue. Why? He had no idea, but he didn't think it was simply a kind gesture on her part. "W-who are you? What do you want?"

She gripped his arm and steered him toward a dark blue SUV. "We need to talk."

Talk? His paranoid instincts from the time he'd spent living on the streets came rushing back to him. She was even more beautiful up close, but that didn't mean anything. He dug in his heels and roughly shook off her hand. "No way, lady. I'm not going anywhere with you."

"Trent, I have reason to believe the guy who attacked you is no ordinary mugger." She stepped closer, tipping her head back to meet his gaze. For a tiny thing, she'd packed a wallop.

No ordinary mugger? The crime rate in Nashville was such that he found it difficult to believe. Lots of petty crime and worse happened every day. Why would tonight be any different?

"We need to talk," she repeated sternly.

He swallowed hard and eyed her warily. The way she referred to him by name was alarming. As if she knew a lot about him when he didn't know squat about her. "About what?"

There was a long moment of silence before she said, "Jimmy Woodrow's murder."

Murder. The word hit him square in the chest with the impact of a bullet. He staggered back a step, wondering if he'd misheard her. Maybe he was losing his grip on reality. It wouldn't be a surprise to realize the secrets he'd never voiced had instead slowly and surely eaten away at him, causing him to go quietly insane.

Even the role he'd played in the night of the fire when he and his foster siblings had escaped the Preacher's cabin didn't compare to what had transpired with Jimmy. Not for the first time, it occurred to Trent he never should have left his foster brother Cooper behind in Gatlinburg.

He never should have come to Nashville at all.

"Please, Trent. I promise I only want to talk."

He shouldn't trust her. He had learned to trust no one, except maybe Cooper, who was still living in Gatlinburg and was of no help to him now. In fact, Trent had ignored his foster brother's phone call a couple of weeks ago, too embarrassed to respond. But that didn't matter right now.

"Who are you?" he demanded.

"My name is Serena Jerash." She paused as if waiting for him to recognize her.

He didn't.

"Why do you care about Jimmy?" he asked harshly.

Her gaze was shadowed in the darkness, impossible to read. "I'm a friend of his. And I just want to talk to you, nothing more."

Yeah, she kept saying that, but he wasn't buying it, not for one hot minute. She must have known he had been there the night Jimmy had died. It was the only explanation.

The steamy September night closed in on him, stealing his breath. He struggled to remain focused, ignoring the keen, desperate desire to go back inside for a shot and a beer, followed by another and another until he could no longer see Jimmy's blank stare in his mind. Yet Trent knew the relief would only be temporary. Staying sober was the only way to survive. He gathered every ounce of willpower he possessed. "Lady, I don't know who you are or what you're up to, but I'm not going anywhere with you." He turned away.

"There's a restaurant that's open all night about a mile up the road." She hurried after him, putting a hand on his arm. She was persistent, he'd give her that much. "We can talk there. It's a public place but won't be too busy at this time of night."

"Why should I?" He stared at her. "Muggings are not unusual in Nashville, and in case you haven't noticed, we happen to be standing in a rough part of town." He was at the point where he couldn't afford to be picky when it came to places willing to hire him to sing and play his guitar. He took any and all gigs he could get. Even then, he was barely making ends meet.

"Because the same person who killed Jimmy Woodrow is likely coming after you."

That blunt statement stopped him cold. "Are you a cop?"

"No. As I said, I just want to talk."

His thoughts whirled. He shouldn't talk to her. To anyone. Trent knew the best thing he could do was to get as far away from the blonde as possible. Yet she'd been at his last few gigs. And would likely show up next Friday here at the Thirsty Saloon to see him.

Unless he blew off the gig, which he was in no position to do.

"Please, Trent." Her low husky voice had him wondering if she was a singer. It would explain her interest in Jimmy's death.

His murder?

His curiosity got the better of him, and he capitulated. "Fine. I'll see you at Connie's Café." Without saying anything more, he twisted out of her grip and walked to his rusty and badly dented Ford truck. After sliding his guitar off his shoulders, he stored it in the back seat, then climbed in behind the wheel. Glancing through the driver's side window, he noticed Serena Jerash hurried to her much newer and nicer SUV.

Against his better judgment, Trent waited for her to pull out of the parking lot before following behind. The ride to Connie's Café didn't take long, and he seriously considered driving past once they'd reached their destination.

But he pulled in and parked beside her, hoping he wasn't making a giant mistake.

SERENA HALF EXPECTED Trent to make a run for it, but to her surprise, he parked his battered truck right beside her. He waited for her to emerge from the vehicle first before pushing open his door to accompany her inside.

Her hands were sore from where she'd struck the assailant before he'd dropped the knife and taken off. She'd been relieved there hadn't been a need to pull her gun. She'd seriously considered using it because going after the guy might have given her an indication of who had hired him. Yet sticking close to Trent Atkins had seemed the better choice.

For now.

Because of the late hour, there was no hostess on duty. Serena led the way to a booth in the back corner of the café. Trent's expression was grim as he slid in across from her.

The musician was a very good-looking man, or he would be if he smiled more often. Trent was also very talented, although her father's best friend's son, Jimmy Woodrow, had been even more so. The entire family knew Jimmy was brimming with talent, a shining star, one whose light had been extinguished far too soon.

As a private investigator, Serena had been hired by Jimmy's father to uncover the truth about his son's murder. Granted, the ME's report had deemed Jimmy's death to be undetermined, mostly because his tox screen had tested positive for alcohol and cocaine. Not enough to kill him, however, but still an indicator of his lifestyle. One that may have contributed to his demise.

Yet the rumor amongst the cops who'd responded to the scene was that something shady had happened that night. Without witnesses or much to go on, the investigation had stalled and became dormant.

There was a fair amount of crime in Nashville, always

another murder to deal with. And the indeterminate conclusion from the ME didn't offer much clarity either.

Trent continued to stare at her, clearly not willing to start the conversation. Once the server had brought waters and had taken their orders, she leaned forward leaning her elbows on the table.

"I know Jimmy Woodrow was no saint. He was an extremely talented musician, but he also partied a little too much."

Trent didn't so much as blink. She took that to mean she hadn't told him anything he didn't already know. Which was true. As Jimmy's lead guitarist, she knew Trent had more knowledge of those parties than she did.

"I don't know if you realize the medical examiner listed the cause of Jimmy's death as indeterminate."

"You said murder." It was the first thing he'd said since leaving the parking lot at the Thirsty Saloon.

"Yes, because I believe he was murdered." She didn't want to tell him too much, but she needed his cooperation, now more than ever. "And I know you were with him that night."

If she hadn't been watching him so closely, she might have missed the nearly imperceptible flinch. "You're wrong."

"No, I'm not." She'd been working on this case for several weeks and had learned from another member of the now broken-up band that Jimmy and Trent had been very tight. It didn't make sense that he wouldn't have been there that night.

Trent sat back in the booth. "You're right about the fact that I was at the hotel for a while after the gig. We typically got together to celebrate finishing up a good run, and that night was the one in which we opened for Luke Bryan, which was huge. We all knew that night was our trip to the big leagues, so of course we were pumped. But I didn't stay overnight. I left at four in the morning."

"Drunk?" she asked pointedly.

He shrugged. "Rideshares are the best invention since sliced bread. No reason to drink and drive."

Interesting that he hadn't denied drinking. Then again, useless to deny something so easily proved as the two former band members she'd spoken to had mentioned how much Trent liked to drink. And how much he and Jimmy had partied that night he'd ended up dead in the hotel room.

Watching Trent for the past few nights, she'd noticed he'd only drank water with fresh slices of lemon. Which didn't mean anything, he could have turned into a closet drinker, hiding his addiction from the prying eyes of the world.

But not from God.

Serena prayed for guidance as she regarded him thoughtfully. "That isn't exactly the story I've heard, but we can set that issue aside for now. The real question here is who killed Jimmy? And why has that same person decided to come after you?"

A flash of impatience crossed his features. "Are you some sort of journalist? Because you're pretty good at making up stories. There's no proof Jimmy was murdered, and there's no reason on earth the killer would come after me. Jimmy died three months ago. I'm pretty sure the Nashville police department has already stuck his death deep into their cold case file."

She had to admit he was right about that. With no new leads to go on, the Nashville PD had moved on. The case wasn't necessarily in the cold case file, but it sure wasn't being actively pursued.

But it would be once she found the evidence they needed to keep moving the case forward.

"Why would someone attack you?" She lifted a brow. "Have you made someone mad? Cheated with a married woman? Owe someone money? What?"

He frowned. "None of the above. You're making up stories again. That attack was a random thing." His gaze narrowed. "Unless, of course, you're the one who set it up. I've been never attacked by anyone until tonight. And you've been to my last few gigs."

Again, she couldn't help being impressed because she would have thought the exact same thing. And she had no reason to be paranoid, unlike Trent.

Their server brought their breakfast meals, then left them alone. Serena bowed her head and silently thanked God for the food and for guiding her to Trent in time to help him escape the hoodie assailant.

When she lifted her head, Trent was staring at her oddly. "What was that?" he asked.

"A prayer." She didn't understand why he was confused. "Considering the earlier attack, we have a lot to be thankful for."

"Yeah, right." His snide tone surprised her. Trent had been suspicious, blunt, confused, curious, and skeptical, but he hadn't been downright rude.

"I take it you don't believe in God." She picked up her fork and cut into her omelet. Something about eating after midnight always made her want to order breakfast. Apparently, Trent felt the same.

"No, although I lived with the devil for about five years." He turned his attention to his meal, oblivious to her shocked expression.

"I'm sorry to hear that." The words were grossly inadequate. "That must have been terrible."

"Yeah." Trent lapsed back into silence, concentrating on his meal as if his life depended on it. Which made her wonder about what he'd done before joining up with the Jimmy Woodrow Band. Not that Trent's personal life should matter to her one way or the other.

Unless it had some sort of bearing on what had triggered Jimmy's murder. But somehow she didn't think so. No, Trent had been the lead guitarist, but whoever had killed Jimmy had a personal reason to do so.

Her father's friend Allan Woodrow had maintained an overly positive view toward his talented son. He'd acted as if the drinking and drugs were smears on Jimmy's good name by those who were jealous of his ability.

But that was not the picture Serena was uncovering through her investigation. Granted, the two band members could have been exaggerating, but she didn't think so. Jimmy had been wild when it came to women and having fun. Finding his tox screen had contained alcohol and cocaine had only confirmed what Jed Matson and Dave Jacoby had told her. Whatever had transpired that fateful night, she was certain Jimmy had been too impaired to fight back or escape.

"Do you remember seeing anything suspicious the night Jimmy died?"

He glanced sharply at her. "No."

She refused to be deterred. "I need you to think back on that night, on what was going on before you left. Any fighting? Arguing? Anything remotely unusual?"

"There was nothing to fight about, we'd just opened for a big-time star, and we were celebrating." He stuck stubbornly to his story. "We drank too much and probably got too loud. I vaguely remember the hotel security coming to ask us to be quiet."

That was something she hadn't heard before. "Do you remember what time that was?"

"No." He dropped his gaze to his empty plate, which he'd devoured in record time, then he dug into his jeans pocket for some cash. "Sorry I can't be of more help, but I need to get home."

Serena didn't want him to leave. "What if I told you that Jed and Dave remembered there was an argument?"

His gaze snapped up to hers. "When did you speak to them?"

"Last week." She eyed him steadily. "Sounds as if you and Jimmy were not in agreement about something, they both mentioned some harsh words between you."

His cheeks flushed, and he tossed a twenty-dollar bill onto the table and stood. "You're mistaken. We were celebrating. Frankly, I don't appreciate you treating me as a suspect. I guess you lied to me about being a cop after all." He stalked away, his long stride taking him quickly across the restaurant.

She winced, realizing she hadn't handled that very well. She pulled out some cash and added it to his before hurrying after him.

But Trent was already in his truck, the engine rumbling to life. She hopped into her SUV and followed. She knew where he lived because she'd tailed him home from his gig last weekend. It was a hole-in-the-wall apartment, a far cry from the plush Grand Ole Opry Hotel where they'd stayed the night of Jimmy's murder.

Which was another reason she didn't believe he'd left at four in the morning. Why would he ditch the swank surroundings for a tiny apartment?

He wouldn't. No one would.

Trent Atkins was hiding something. He wasn't necessarily a suspect, but he was definitely hiding something.

For one thing, he wasn't nearly as forthcoming as Jed and Dave had been. They'd relished talking about the old days and had seemed genuinely upset about Jimmy's death.

They'd also seemed intrigued by the idea of their band leader being murdered, offering up dozens of possibilities.

Including one in which Trent and Jimmy had argued over a woman.

In her humble opinion, both men were handsome enough to hold their own in that regard. Add that to being in a band and she found it hard to imagine either of them resorting to fighting over a woman.

Then again, they'd both likely been drinking and doing drugs, so who knows what had gone through their minds?

Trent slowed near a tavern, but then speeded up again. She wondered if he'd given up on the drinking and drugs in the months since Jimmy's death.

She decided to pray that God would guide him on the road to recovery.

When she saw Trent pull into the small parking lot outside his shabby apartment building, she drove past the place, but then pulled over to the side of the road. Getting out of the SUV, she headed back on foot. From her angle, she could see Trent sitting behind the wheel and staring out through the windshield for several long moments.

What was he thinking? She'd have given a hundred bucks for his thoughts. Was he remembering the night Jimmy had died? Jed Matson who was a drummer and Dave Jacoby who played the keyboard were both members of a new band called the Bootleggers. Not exactly an original name for Tennessee and Kentucky, but they seemed to be doing okay. Nowhere near as well as Jimmy Woodrow, but not bad.

So why had Trent struck out on his own?

Serena had more questions than answers after the brief time she'd spent with Trent. And she was keenly aware of the fact that she'd provided far more information than he'd given in return.

Trent pushed open his driver's side door. Something hit the ground, and he bent over to retrieve it at the exact moment a gunshot rang out, shattering the driver's side window of his truck. He hit the ground and shimmied beneath the vehicle.

"Trent! Stay down!" Serena pulled her weapon and crouched down behind a parked car. Using her phone, she called 911 to report the gunfire as her gaze searched for the shooter.

No way was this second attempt on Trent's life a coincidence.

In a few short hours, someone had tried to kill him *twice*.

And with a guilty flush, she couldn't help but wonder if her finding and questioning him had caused this to happen.